THE BOBBSEY TWINS
SEARCH FOR THE GREEN ROOSTER

The day Mr. Machado's strange letter arrives from Portugal marks the beginning of an exciting trip and a baffling mystery for the Bobbsey twins to solve. Mr. Machado has written to ask the whole Bobbsey family to come to Portugal and pick up a rare and valuable gift he has for them. But the second page of his letter is missing, and the Bobbseys have no idea what the gift might be. The only clue lies in the words *galo verde*.

To make everything even more puzzling, when the Bobbseys arrive in Lisbon, they find that Mr. Machado has left the country! With some difficulty, the twins locate his housekeeper, who says there was indeed a package left for them, but it has been stolen from the house during a recent wave of burglaries in the neighborhood.

The Bobbseys don't speak Portuguese, but they manage to make themselves understood. With the help of some new little Portuguese friends, Bert and Nan, and even Flossie and Freddie, track down one clue after another and have many adventures—some amusing and some spooky.

In the end, it is little Flossie Bobbsey who, quite by accident, stumbles upon the secret passageway which, in turn, leads the twins to the hidden treasure.

THE BOBBSEY TWINS BOOKS
By Laura Lee Hope

Nan waved the paper in the air

The Bobbsey Twins' Search for the Green Rooster

By

LAURA LEE HOPE

GROSSET & DUNLAP

Publishers   *New York*

PRINTED IN THE UNITED STATES OF AMERICA

The Bobbsey Twins' Search for the Green Rooster

CONTENTS

CHAPTER I

THE MYSTERIOUS LETTER

"DADDY! Here's a letter and it looks 'citing!"

Blond Flossie Bobbsey, her blue eyes sparkling, ran to her father in the dining room. She handed him an envelope.

"Wow!" exclaimed Freddie. "Look at that sharp-looking stamp on it! Where's the letter from?" the little boy asked. He looked very much like Flossie, who was his twin.

Nan and Bert, the dark-haired, twelve-year-old Bobbsey twins, laughed. "Give Dad a chance to open it," said Bert.

Smiling, tall and handsome Mr. Bobbsey said, "This is from Portugal." He slit the envelope quickly and took out two sheets. He began to read and then looked up, puzzled. "The second page is missing!" he exclaimed. "Just the first and third are here."

1

"Are you sure, Dick?" asked Mrs. Bobbsey. The twins' mother was pretty and had a sweet smile.

The family was seated at the dining table in their comfortable house in Lakeport. Mr. Bobbsey had come home to lunch from his lumberyard on the shore of nearby Lake Metoka.

Mr. Bobbsey searched the envelope carefully, but it was empty. "Very strange," he remarked.

"Is the letter from a friend of yours, Dad?" Nan asked.

"Yes. Mr. Machado, who lives in Portugal."

"What does he say?" Bert asked his father.

Mr. Bobbsey turned back to the first page of the letter. "He is closing his old family home outside of Lisbon and selling the contents. He's moving to Brazil. His house is called *Quinta do San Francisco.*" Mr. Bobbsey looked up from the letter. "I believe the Portuguese word *quinta* means farm."

Just then a stout, jolly-looking colored woman came into the room carrying a flaky pie.

"Boy! That looks good, Dinah!" Bert exclaimed.

Dinah and her husband, Sam Johnson, had lived in an apartment on the third floor of the Bobbsey house for many years. Dinah helped Mrs. Bobbsey with the housework, while Sam worked at the lumberyard.

As Mrs. Bobbsey served the dessert, Bert turned to his father. "Did Mr. Machado say anything else interesting?"

Mr. Bobbsey winked at his wife. "Rather interesting," he agreed. "Mr. Machado wants us to come to Portugal!"

Freddie and Flossie clapped in excitement. "Are we going, Daddy?" Flossie asked.

"Well, my little fat fairy and my little fat fireman," Mr. Bobbsey began. These were his favorite nicknames for the chubby younger twins. Flossie loved to dance and Freddie often declared he was going to be a fireman when he grew up.

"Mr. Machado wants to give us something of his which is very old and very valuable," said their father. "And he would like us to come to the *quinta* and pick it up. I don't know what it is. He evidently wrote a description of the article on the missing second page!"

"Please tell us what the third page says," Nan requested.

Mr. Bobbsey held up the sheet of paper. "There are only two words on it besides Mr. Machado's final greeting and signature. They are *galo verde.*"

"What do the words mean, Dick?" Mrs. Bobbsey asked.

"I don't know. Bert, how about you and Nan

going to the library this afternoon and looking them up?"

"What do you s'pose the present is?" Flossie wondered.

"I can't even guess!" said Nan, but her eyes danced. "It's a real mystery!"

She and the other Bobbsey twins loved mysteries and had solved many of them. In THE GREEK HAT MYSTERY they discovered a strange note in a fur hat and from it were able to track down some thieves in Greece.

"Anyhow," said Mrs. Bobbsey, "Mr. Machado is very nice to give us something. I think he is grateful for the help you gave him when he was here in Lakeport, Dick."

The Portuguese man had come to Lakeport on business the year before. Because of his lack of English he had been about to make a grave financial mistake when Mr. Bobbsey had come to his rescue. Mr. Machado had not forgotten.

"*Are* we going to Portugal?" Bert asked.

Mr. Bobbsey laughed. "Yes. As a matter of fact, I had planned the trip before I received his letter," he said. "I have a commission to meet a business friend over there and perhaps buy some cork oak trees for which Portugal is famous. I thought it would be nice to take you twins and your mother. I'll write Mr. Machado that we'll be glad to pick up our present from him."

"Hooray!" Freddie shouted. "We're really and truly going to Portugal!"

When luncheon was over Bert said, "Come on, Nan. Let's hurry to the library and find out what *galo verde* means!"

At the library Nan took a Portuguese-English dictionary from the shelves while Bert found a book about Portugal.

Hurriedly Nan leafed through the pages until she came to the G's. The next moment she began to giggle. "Guess what *galo verde* means, Bert!"

"What?"

"Green rooster!"

"Green rooster!" Bert repeated, puzzled. "Mr. Machado can't be giving us a green rooster!"

"We'll just have to wait until we get to Portugal to find out," Nan observed with a sigh. Then she looked over at Bert's book. "What have you found out?"

Bert told his sister that Portugal was a seafaring nation. Portuguese sailors made many voyages of discovery in the fifteenth century. They had explored the west coast of Africa and sailed around that continent to India.

"I'm glad we're going there," Bert declared. "The Portuguese must be very brave people."

Later when Bert and Nan told the other Bobbseys what they had learned at the library,

Flossie laughed. "It's a cock-a-doodle-doo mystery!" she cried. "We're going to find a green rooster!"

"Are there still sailors in Portugal?" Freddie asked. "Can we go sailing?"

"I don't know about that," replied Mr. Bobbsey, "but next to the making of cork products, fishing is the greatest industry. Perhaps you can fish while we're there."

Freddie's eyes shone. He loved to fish.

The next afternoon the little boy ran to Bert, who was reading on the front porch. "Let's go fishing!" he proposed. "We ought to practice for Portugal."

Since both the boys could swim they often fished together on Lake Metoka. There was a rowboat at the lumberyard dock which Bert was allowed to take out. The brothers left the house.

A short time later Freddie climbed into the boat with the two fishing rods. Bert shoved the craft down to the water, jumped in and took up the oars. As he pulled away from shore, a big fish leaped from the water ahead. The sun shone on his silvery body a second and then he was gone.

"Row over there, Bert!" Freddie said excitedly. "I'd like to catch him!"

Obligingly Bert steered the rowboat toward the spot while Freddie let out his line. The sinker carried it far below the surface. Suddenly the line grew taut.

"I've got him!" Freddie shouted, beginning to reel in furiously.

But the fish was strong and struggled desperately to free itself. A sudden jerk on the line made Freddie lose his balance. He tumbled toward the side of the boat.

"Whoa there, pardner!" Bert cried. He let go the oars and grabbed Freddie by the ankle just as he was about to fall overboard.

"Thanks, Bert!" Freddie gasped. He lifted his

rod. The line had gone slack. "I lost my big fish!" the little boy said sadly.

"Maybe you'll hook another," Bert consoled him.

In the meantime Nan and Flossie had gone down to the business section of Lakeport to do an errand for Mrs. Bobbsey.

As they came out of the bookstore Nan said, "Would you like some ice cream, Floss? Mother gave me money for a treat."

"Goody," said Flossie, skipping along beside her sister. "Let's go to the Soda Shop."

The Soda Shop was a favorite meeting place for the young people of Lakeport. The ice cream there was homemade and delicious.

When the Bobbsey girls walked in, they saw two friends at a table near the door—Nellie Parks and Charlie Mason. Both Nellie and Charlie were in the same class at school as Bert and Nan.

"Hi, Nan!" Nellie called. "Come sit with us." The pretty, blond girl beckoned toward two empty seats.

After the Bobbseys gave their orders, Charlie asked teasingly, "Solved any mysteries lately?"

"We have a cock-a-doodle-doo mystery to solve!" Flossie piped up, her blue eyes sparkling mischievously.

"A what?" Nellie asked.

Two boys seated on stools at the counter turned around and listened as Nan and Flossie told about Mr. Machado and his mysterious gift.

"So we're going to Portugal to find the green rooster!" Nan concluded with a laugh.

"A green rooster!" one of the boys at the counter said sneeringly. "There isn't any such thing!"

"I know that, Danny!" Nan declared. "But Mr. Machado's letter said something about a green rooster, so we're going to find out what he meant."

Danny Rugg and his friend Jack Westley were also in Nan's class, but they were not very well liked by the other children. They were bullies and played mean tricks, especially on the Bobbseys.

"Crazy kids!" Danny muttered as he and Jack slipped from the stools and left the shop.

"That Danny!" Charlie looked disgusted. "He's a nut!"

"I think your trip sounds fabulous!" said Nellie to the twins.

Charlie added, "I'll bet you'll find the green rooster!"

"We're sure going to try," said Nan. Soon she and Flossie left.

That evening Mrs. Bobbsey came into the living room where the twins were working a jigsaw puzzle. "Your father and I are going out," she said. "Dinah and Sam are upstairs if you need anything."

"All right, Mother," Nan replied. "Have a nice time!"

"Yes, have a nice time!" the others chorused.

An hour later Bert had just succeeded in placing the last piece in the puzzle when the children heard a frantic barking from the front lawn.

"That's Waggo," Freddie declared. Waggo was their frisky fox terrier. "What's he so excited about?"

"I'll see." Bert hurried to open the front door. "For Pete's sake!" he exclaimed.

Tied to one of the porch posts was a squawking rooster, and around its neck was a bright green handkerchief!

CHAPTER II

A STRANGE GUEST

AT Bert's cry the other twins ran to the door. They burst into laughter when they saw the rooster. Waggo continued to bark and leap around.

"Wherever did he come from?" Flossie cried.

Nan shook her head. "I can't imagine, but bring the rooster inside, Bert," she urged.

Her twin untied the cord holding the bird. With the still-squawking rooster safely tucked under his arm, Bert came back into the living room.

Flossie was jumping up and down excitedly. "Something's pinned to the handkerchief!" she cried.

Nan reached over and pulled off the piece of paper. "There's writing on it!"

"What does it say?" Freddie asked. "Is the rooster a present for us?"

Nan read the note: HERE IS YOUR GREEN ROOSTER. WHY GO TO PORTUGAL?

"Is it signed?" asked Bert.

"No, but this is Danny Rugg's writing. He heard Flossie and me telling Nellie and Charlie about Mr. Machado's green rooster."

"What shall we do with the rooster?" Nan asked. "We can't take the poor thing back to Danny now."

"Let's keep our visitor in the kitchen. He'll be safe there," said Bert and carried him inside.

The next morning the children were dressing when they heard a wild shriek from the kitchen. All the Bobbseys ran out into the upstairs hall.

"Something's happened to Dinah!" Mrs. Bobbsey said. She and her husband started to run down the stairs.

"I know! It's the rooster!" Freddie cried, doubling over with laughter. "She's seen the rooster!"

The twins hurried after their parents, explaining what had happened the night before. By the time they reached the kitchen, Dinah had recovered from her fright.

"Who put that old chicken in my kitchen?" she asked indignantly. The family had a hard time keeping straight faces.

"Danny Rugg brought us the rooster," Nan

told her. "Bert will take him back after break-fast."

He and Nan ate quickly, then started for the Ruggs' house. Bert carried the rooster under his arm. Nan rang the Ruggs' doorbell, but there was no answer.

"Everybody's out," Nan said. "Now what shall we do?"

Bert pointed to Danny's bicycle, which stood against the side of the house. "We'll tie our friend there and leave a note," he decided.

The long string was still attached to the bird's foot. Bert quickly tied the other end to a spoke of the bicycle wheel. Then he pulled out a little notebook and pencil from his pocket.

"What shall I write?" he asked.

The two thought for a while, and finally decided to say: THE ROOSTER ISN'T GREEN ENOUGH! WE'RE GOING TO PORTUGAL TO FIND THE REAL ONE!

Bert printed the words, and Nan pinned the paper to the green handkerchief. This they tied to the wheel of the bicycle.

When Bert and Nan reached home, their mother was waiting for them. "Nellie Parks just phoned," she said. "Will you call her, Nan?"

A few minutes later Nan came from the tele-phone and said to the other twins, "Nellie is having a good-by party for us tomorrow afternoon. We're to come in Portuguese costumes."

"Goody!" Flossie clapped her hands. "That will be fun!"

Up in the attic the Bobbseys had a trunk where they kept all sorts of clothes which could be used for costumes. The four children ran to the third floor and rummaged through the collection. The girls finally decided on full skirts of bright printed cotton, and white, low-necked blouses.

"What are you going to wear, Bert?" Flossie asked.

Her brother looked mysterious. "I have an idea. First I'm going to the library and read up on something."

Later that afternoon Bert returned with a book. "I'll be Prince Henry the Navigator," he announced. "The prince was really great! He set up the first school of navigation in Europe. That's why the Portuguese were such successful explorers."

He showed the other children a picture of the prince, who was born in the latter part of the fourteenth century. It portrayed a solemn man who wore a large hat with a broad, turned-up brim and a long, full coat with a narrow stand-up collar.

Mrs. Bobbsey looked at the picture and said, "I think I can help you, Bert. I have an old hat and a coat almost like Prince Henry's!"

"That'll be keen, Mother. Thanks," said Bert.

Freddie looked downcast. While the others were discussing their costumes he wandered down to the kitchen.

"What you got such a long face about?" Dinah asked him.

Sadly Freddie told her the other three children had costumes to wear to Nellie's party, but he could not think of one.

"Why don't you be that green rooster you're all talkin' about?" Dinah suggested with a chuckle.

Freddie beamed. "That's a super idea, Dinah!" he cried. "Will you help me?"

"I sure will!" she declared. "You come to the attic with me right now and we'll start!"

Opening the trunk once more, Freddie pulled out a green cloth helmet Bert had worn in a school play. "Hey, how about this?" he asked.

"That's fine," Dinah said approvingly. "And I'll make you a dandy rooster's comb out of this." She picked up a square of bright red paper.

Freddie lifted out a large straw hat decorated with two yellow ostrich plumes. "Would these do for tail feathers?" he asked.

Dinah chuckled. "Why not? They *were* part of a bird's tail!"

The next afternoon the twins assembled in their costumes to let Mrs. Bobbsey and Dinah admire them. Bert looked very dignified as the prince in the large hat and long coat, while Nan and Flossie were gay in their peasant costumes.

They all laughed and applauded when Freddie appeared. The red paper comb stuck up jauntily from the green helmet. Freddie had put on a green shirt and shorts and Dinah had pinned the yellow feathers to his back.

"You're a real green rooster!" Bert told him.

Freddie strutted around proudly, crying, "Cock-a-doodle-doo!"

When they arrived at Nellie's house, the Bobbsey twins found her in a full black skirt with a brightly embroidered apron and a tight little black jacket over a white blouse.

Charlie wore navy shorts and a white shirt and had wound a red cummerbund around his waist. Susie Larker and Teddy Blake, who were Freddie's and Flossie's special friends, also had on bright costumes like those that Portuguese dancers wear.

"I invited Danny and Jack," Nellie confided to Nan, "but they said they wouldn't dress up."

"Here they come now," said Nan as the two boys walked into the yard.

Bert called out to Danny, "How's the rooster business today?"

Danny's face grew red. "Aw, you Bobbseys and your silly mysteries."

The twins laughed, which made Danny even more uncomfortable. Now Nellie started the record player, and a lively tune poured out. "I thought it would be fun to have a march first," she told her guests. The children in their colorful costumes fell into line and began to walk around the yard.

Danny, a sly smile on his face, edged over to the side of the house where the faucet which controlled the ground sprinkler system jutted out. He gave the faucet a quick turn.

The next second jets of water sprang up all over the yard. The children scattered, squealing.

With jeering laughs, Danny and Jack raced from the yard. "Sissies!" Danny yelled back. He and Jack sped on down the street and disappeared around the corner.

"I'm glad they're gone." Flossie spoke up. "We'll have more fun."

After a few fast games of tag, the children trooped into the house where they had ice cream and cake. When the time came to leave, the young guests told Nellie it was a wonderful party in spite of Danny's mean trick.

A few days later the Bobbseys flew to New York where they boarded a huge jet plane for Portugal. Hours later they landed near its capital city.

Nan noticed a large sign *Lisboa* over the

Jets of water sprang up all over the yard

airport building. She was puzzled. "I thought the city was Lis*bon*," she said.

"Remember we're in Portugal now," her father said. "That's the way the Portuguese spell the name."

The airport was not far from the city and Mr. Bobbsey engaged a car to take the family to the hotel where he had made reservations.

They drove along a broad avenue lined with palm trees. The buildings they passed were painted in pastel colors with wrought iron balconies across the front. In the distance more buildings could be seen covering the hills.

"You know Lisbon is built on seven hills," Mr. Bobbsey explained.

Soon the car turned onto another wide boulevard with a park running down the center. "This is the Avenida Liberdade," Mr. Bobbsey said. "Our hotel is on this street."

Shortly they stopped in front of a large modern hotel. After registering, the Bobbseys were taken upstairs to their suite.

"When are we going to see the green rooster?" Flossie asked as she saw her mother begin to unpack.

"I'll telephone Mr. Machado now," Mr. Bobbsey replied. He picked up the room phone and asked the operator to put in a call for the Quinta do San Francisco.

In a few minutes the bell rang. Mr. Bobbsey picked up the instrument and listened. A look of bewilderment came over his face.

"Thank you," he said, and put down the phone.

Then he turned to his family. "Mr. Machado's telephone has been discontinued!" he reported.

CHAPTER III

PUZZLING THEFTS

"DISCONTINUED!" Bert repeated. "You mean Mr. Machado doesn't live there any more?"

Mr. Bobbsey looked worried. "He may have left for Brazil, but he didn't say he was going so soon."

"Can't we see the green rooster?" Flossie wailed.

"I don't know," her father replied. "It's strange that Mr. Machado didn't let me know that he wouldn't be here."

Mr. Bobbsey thought for a minute, then made a decision. "I'll hire a car, and we'll drive out there tomorrow to see what's going on."

"Goody!" Flossie cried. "Then we can find the green rooster!"

Arrangements were made to have an automobile delivered to the hotel the following

21

morning. When it arrived the children were surprised to see that it was not so large as theirs at home. Mr. Bobbsey explained that many European roads were too narrow and winding for the big American cars.

Mr. and Mrs. Bobbsey and Flossie got in front while the older twins and Freddie climbed into the rear seat.

Mr. Bobbsey had received directions from the manager at the hotel on how to reach the Quinta do San Francisco. He told his family that the quinta was near the small village of Magros.

"We go through the towns of Estoril and Cascais," he said. "All this area is full of estates and large homes of wealthy people. Many rich refugees from other countries and a few ex-kings have settled here."

"I'd like to see a king," said Nan, peering eagerly out the window. But she saw no one.

The road was narrow and wound through fruit orchards and olive groves. The Bobbseys passed many carts and wagons drawn by donkeys or horses. Occasionally a truck sped by, but there were very few private cars.

"Look!" Nan called out as they rounded a bend.

Walking along the side of the road were two women. They were dressed in full skirts and white blouses decorated with lace. On their

heads they carried great trays of garden vege-
tables. The children waved and the women gave
pleased smiles.

"They're taking produce into the city to sell, I
suppose," Mrs. Bobbsey remarked.

A short while later the road widened as Mr.
Bobbsey drove through the resort towns of
Estoril and Cascais, which stretched along the
ocean shore. Then he turned inland and once
more the road grew narrow.

The car sped up a slight grade and around a
curve, then swerved violently. Directly ahead
was a cart piled high with wicker crates of
chickens and pulled by a donkey. The donkey
was ambling along on the wrong side of the
road.

Beep! Beep!

At the sound of Mr. Bobbsey's horn, the cart
driver pulled over but not quickly enough. The
front bumper of the car struck the corner of the
cart. It tilted, and the crates fell out onto the
road. Several of the flimsy crates came open and
immediately the air was full of squawking
birds!

"Now I've done it!" said Mr. Bobbsey as he
pulled to the side of the road and stopped.

"We'll help you get the chickens!" Nan called
to the farmer, who had climbed down from his
seat and was frantically trying to catch them.

"We'll help you get the chickens!" Nan called

The children jumped from the car and ran
back to the cart. The frightened birds tried to
escape into the field, but the four Bobbseys were
too quick for them. One by one, the twins managed to grab the chickens and put them back into
the crates. The farmer soon had the latches
fastened again and set the crates up on the cart.

In sign language, Mr. Bobbsey told the man
how sorry he was to have caused the trouble and
handed him several bills.

A broad smile broke over the farmer's face.
"Obrigado, obrigado!" he cried.

"I guess that means 'thanks,' " Bert observed.
"We must remember it."

Mr. Bobbsey drove on and presently reached
an intersection in the little village of Magros.
"I'm not sure which road will take us to the
quinta," he said. "I'll see if this boy can tell us."
He stopped the car near a small boy standing to
one side of the street.

"Do you speak English?" Mr. Bobbsey asked
him.

"Não." The boy shook his head.

"Quinta do San Francisco?" Mr. Bobbsey
tried to indicate he wanted directions.

At the words the child looked frightened. He
shook his head again, but this time he seemed to
be warning Mr. Bobbsey.

"Let me try, Dad." Bert leaned forward. He

gave the boy a friendly grin and pointed first in one direction then the other, and raised his eyebrows questioningly. Reluctantly the Portuguese youngster pointed to the right and ran off down the street.

"What was that all about?" Nan asked wonderingly as they rode along. "The boy looked as if he wanted to tell us not to go to the quinta!"

"I hope nothing is wrong!" Mrs. Bobbsey said nervously.

"We'll soon know," Mr. Bobbsey said. "Here we are."

Ahead, the children could see a large pink stucco house set in a garden. A concrete wall about six feet high enclosed the property. As the car drew nearer they noticed a wrought iron entrance gate. Over it was an arch with the words: Quinta do San Francisco.

Mr. Bobbsey stopped the car. Bert jumped out and rang a bell set into one of the gate posts. They could hear a jangling sound in the distance, but no one came to let them in.

"I'm afraid no one is here, Dick," Mrs. Bobbsey remarked.

"Maybe there's another entrance." Nan, followed by the younger twins, joined Bert. "Let's walk around the wall and see!"

The children were gone for some time. When they returned they reported there was no other gate and that the whole place was deserted.

"Maybe we can find someone in Magros who speaks English," Nan suggested, "and can tell us where Mr. Machado is."

Mr. Bobbsey drove back to town and stopped in front of a low building which appeared to be the post office. Bert went in. In a few minutes he was back, smiling.

"The postmaster speaks a little English," he said. "Mr. Machado's housekeeper, Maria, lives down this street. She can help us."

Maria proved to be a pleasant woman with black hair which she wore in braids wound over each ear. She introduced them to her son Antonio. He was a bright-looking boy about Bert's age.

"Tony, he speak English," Maria said proudly. "He learn from *o senhor* Machado!"

Mr. Bobbsey introduced his family. Maria and Tony bowed politely to each one. Then, with Tony interpreting, Mr. Bobbsey explained that they had received a letter from Mr. Machado telling of a gift he wished them to have.

"*Sim,* yes," said Tony. "*O senhor* had to leave for Brazil. He tell us your package at quinta. If Sr. Bobbsey not come to Portugal within month my mother must mail to America."

"Is it a green rooster?" Flossie asked with a giggle.

Tony and Maria looked puzzled. *"Galo verde?"* Tony repeated. "We do not know what gift is but do not think it could be green rooster!"

Everyone laughed. Maria motioned the Bobbseys toward the door. "We go quinta!" she said shyly.

They all managed to squeeze into the car. Maria got in front with Mr. and Mrs. Bobbsey while the five children crowded into the rear.

As they rode out of town Bert told Tony about asking directions to the quinta from the boy on the street. "Why was he scared?" Bert queried.

Tony looked worried and spoke to his mother in Portuguese. She replied in a torrent of words which the boy translated for the Bobbseys.

He explained that since Mr. Machado had left for Brazil strange things had been happening at the quinta. People from the neighborhood walking or bicycling past the place at night had reported seeing flickering lights in the house.

"The villagers are afraid to go near quinta now," Tony said.

"Have you told the police about this?" Nan inquired.

"Sim, but *policia* not find anything wrong."

By this time they had reached the quinta. Maria hopped from the car and pulled a large key from her apron pocket. She put it into the lock and the iron gate swung open. The Bobbseys walked inside.

The house was surrounded by a formal garden. Gravel paths stretched between rows of low trimmed bushes and regularly laid out beds of brilliant flowers.

"It's bee-yoo-ti-ful!" cried Flossie.

Maria urged them toward the house. When the Bobbseys entered they saw that it was built around an open air flagstoned patio. In the center was a fountain. Pots of flowering trees stood around the edge of the patio.

"This is lovely!" Nan remarked dreamily.

Proudly Maria showed the Americans through the house. It had not been disturbed, Tony said. The Bobbseys admired the heavy carved furniture, the hand-woven rugs and the bright-colored draperies. On the lower parts of the walls in several rooms were colored tiles in many patterns.

"*Azulejos!*" Maria said when she saw Nan admiring them.

In one room there were several glass cases containing collections of antique china, glass, and little gold and silver figures.

"Look at these, Bert!" Freddie called excitedly. He pointed to a row of small gold filigree sailing ships like those Christopher Columbus used. Each tiny sail was perfectly formed.

"Say! Those are sharp!" Bert exclaimed. "They're like the caravels the Portuguese explorers sailed!"

Seeing the boys' interest, Maria came over and opened the case. She picked up one of the little ships and handed it to Freddie.

As he bent to examine it, Maria gave an exclamation. Tony came running up to her. In reply to a question from him the woman pointed to the case and said a few words in an excited voice.

Tony turned to the boys. "My mother says there should be five of these gold ships. One is gone! They are worth much money. Made by famous man."

He turned one of the little ships over and showed Bert the initials L.V. engraved on the bottom.

Maria had been watching. Suddenly she ran into the adjoining room. Tony hurried after her. Surprised, the Bobbseys followed. Maria darted to a corner, looked for a second, then burst into tears!

"The package Sr. Machado leave for you Bobbseys is also gone!" Tony cried.

CHAPTER IV

THE GOLD SHIP

FREDDIE stared at the Portuguese boy. "You mean somebody took our green rooster?" he asked.

Tony nodded. "A thief has been in house!" he exclaimed. "The little ship and your box—both gone!"

Bert had been thinking. Now he said to Tony, "Will you ask your mother if any strange people came to the quinta before Mr. Machado left?"

Tony relayed the question, then translated the answer. "She says yes, one man come. She not know his name. He wish to buy some things. Sr. Machado say no."

"Does she know where this man lives?"

Again Tony passed on his mother's reply. "No, but she think he work in antique shop in Lisboa. He very angry at Sr. Machado."

"What did he look like?" Nan said.

Tony asked his mother, then told the Bobbseys that the man had been very short and fat with black hair and eyes. She remembered that he ate candy all the time he was talking to Mr. Machado. He had a bag of it in his pocket.

"I wonder if the fat man could have come back and taken the package and ship," Bert surmised.

"Let's see if anything else is missing," Mr. Bobbsey suggested.

Maria and Tony looked carefully through all the rooms and reported that nothing else seemed to be gone.

"You ask many questions," Tony said to Bert. "You think you can find man?"

Bert explained that he and his brother and sisters liked to work on mysteries. "We hope to solve this one."

Tony's dark eyes shone. "I, too, would like to solve mystery. I will help you!"

"Thanks," said Bert. "For a starter, do the words 'green rooster' mean anything to you?"

In halting English Tony explained that the rooster was a very popular figure in Portugal. There was a legend that hundreds of years before, the crowing of a rooster had awakened a garrison of soldiers and thus saved a town from an attack by their enemies, the Moors.

Bert told about the letter his father had received from Mr. Machado. "The second page was missing and the only words on the last page were *galo verde*."

Tony nodded solemnly. "I understand. I will look for green rooster!"

Mr. Bobbsey interrupted. "I think we'd better report these thefts to the police in Magros, then we'll do some sightseeing."

Maria carefully locked the front door and iron gate. Then Mr. Bobbsey drove the group back to town. Tony pointed out the way to the police headquarters. Fortunately the officer in charge spoke English. He told them his name was Dias.

The policeman was disturbed to hear of the thefts at Quinta do San Francisco and made full notes of everything the Bobbseys told him.

"The gold filigree ship should not be too hard to trace," he said, "but the package—it would be easier if I knew what was in it."

Mr. Bobbsey agreed. "All we know about the gift is that a green rooster is connected with it."

"I will inform you if we are able to find it," Officer Dias promised. "We have had several mysterious robberies in this area during the past two weeks. Valuable antiques have been stolen from some of the big estates."

"Perhaps the same thief took the things from Mr. Machado's quinta," Bert suggested.

"It is possible," the officer agreed.

The Bobbseys said good-by to him. Then they left Maria and Tony at their house, and headed out into the country again.

"Where are we going, Daddy?" Flossie piped up.

"I'm hungry!" Freddie complained.

"We'll visit Sintra, which is one of the most attractive towns in Portugal," Mrs. Bobbsey told the children. "I'm sure we'll be able to get some lunch there."

Half an hour later Nan exclaimed, "How lovely!"

The car had rounded a curve, and the town of Sintra had come into view. A cluster of pastel-colored buildings nestled at the foot of a thickly wooded mountain. Its top was covered by mist.

Mr. Bobbsey followed the road to the central square and parked the car. Ahead of them at the top of a steep flight of steps the children saw a huge building of white stucco with a red tile roof.

"Is that a palace?" Nan guessed.

"You're right," said her father.

"What are those things on top?" Bert asked in bewilderment. Two huge inverted cones of stone rose from one section of the roof.

"The original part of this palace was built by the Moors," Mr. Bobbsey explained. "Those are the kitchen chimneys!"

The mention of kitchens reminded Freddie of lunch. "When are we going to eat?" he asked.

"Right now, my little fireman," his father replied. "We'll go through the palace later."

They found a small restaurant on the square and had a simple but tasty meal. Then Freddie and Flossie scampered up the steps in front of the palace. The others followed.

Mr. Bobbsey paid the admission fee, and a guide came to take them through the beautifully decorated rooms. Almost all had walls partly covered with tiles.

"Azulejos," the guide explained. "Very old and very valuable."

The ceilings particularly interested Flossie. In one room it was covered with paintings of magpies; in another, swans. The little girl walked along slowly, her head tilted back as she admired the birds.

Suddenly Flossie found herself alone in the swan room. She was just about to hurry on when a door at the side opened and a short, fat man entered. In his hands he carried a huge green porcelain rooster!

Flossie's eyes widened with excitement. *The green rooster!* She raced into the next room, where the rest of the family was listening to the guide, and ran up to Bert.

"Come!" she whispered, taking his hand. "I've found it!"

"You found what?" Bert asked, as he went back into the swan room with his little sister.

Flossie pointed to the green rooster which the man had placed on a table. Bert looked excited.

"Do you think it's ours?" Flossie asked.

"We'll find out." Bert questioned the man.

"This is an antique soup tureen," the guard explained. "It has been at the palace here for many years."

Flossie whispered to Bert, "Then it's not our rooster."

"Here are others," the guard said. He showed Bert and Flossie several more bowls on a table in the corner of the room. They were in the form of swans, chickens, and crocodiles.

"Their heads come off!" Flossie giggled as the man raised the top of the figures to reveal the bowl for holding soup.

"I'm glad you like them." The man smiled proudly. "Ever since I became a guard here, they have been my special care."

Bert and Flossie thanked the man and hurried to catch up to the others. "I'm sorry that wasn't our green rooster," Flossie said. "It would be fun to have soup in it!"

"Do you think it's ours?" Flossie asked

Nan, Freddie, and their parents were waiting by the car. "There's another palace here we should see," Mr. Bobbsey said. "It's on top of the mountain. The mist has cleared, so we can drive up."

The road was steep and winding. Suddenly, after rounding a curve, the Bobbseys saw the turrets of a castle through the treetops.

"It's like a fairy castle!" Flossie cried.

Finally Mr. Bobbsey drove into a paved court-yard and stopped. The great building of gray stone rose above them. There were slender towers topped with turrets, round projecting bastions to use in time of attack, and squat cupolas.

"A drawbridge!" Freddie exclaimed as they stepped from the car and started toward the entrance. "Do you think someone will pull it up after we get inside?"

Mr. Bobbsey laughed. "I'm afraid the bridge doesn't draw! This Pena Palace was built only a little over a hundred years ago—much too late for a real drawbridge. This one is strictly an imitation."

Flossie shivered. "It looks real!" She took Nan's hand and walked on tiptoe across the bridge and up to the palace entrance.

Inside, the building was full of little tower rooms, circular stone staircases, and great halls. After a while the children grew tired of the guide's lecture and went out onto a balcony that ran along one side of the palace.

"What a super view!" Nan cried.

Far in the distance they could see the city of Lisbon on the banks of the broad Tagus River. Beyond it was the Atlantic Ocean.

While the others admired the panorama, Freddie wandered restlessly along the stone platform. "What a great place to play!" he thought.

A little farther on, the balcony made a right angle turn and grew wider. Freddie noticed something mounted on the railing. He ran forward to examine it.

It was a tiny cannon only about a foot long! Freddie looked at it closely. Every little part was perfect, and the metal was covered with elaborate carving.

"This is neat!" Freddie told himself. "I'll pretend that the enemy is attacking the castle and I'm the only one left to defend it!"

Firmly Freddie grasped the little cannon and bent over to sight along its barrel. The invaders would have no chance, he thought.

The next second, with a puff of smoke and a loud *bang,* the midget cannon discharged!

CHAPTER V

THE UNUSUAL ELEVATOR

THE cannon had fired! Freddie looked around in dismay as tourists rushed outside onto the terrace. Bert ran up to his brother.

"I only touched it, Bert! Honest!" Freddie protested.

"You must have done something to make it go off!" Bert said sternly.

Freddie shook his head, and tears came to his eyes.

At that moment a guard ran up. "Don't blame the little boy!" he said. "The cannon fires automatically when the sun's rays touch it."

While the crowd gathered around, the man explained. When the sun reached a certain place in the sky, its rays passed through a bit of glass on the touchhole of the toy cannon and ignited the powder there.

40

"The little boy just happened to touch the cannon at the exact moment the sun's rays fell on the glass!" the guard said, smiling.

Freddie looked relieved. Mr. Bobbsey took his son's hand and led him away. "We'd better get back to Lisbon before you find a real cannon to set off!" he said teasingly.

Freddie grinned.

The return drive to the city did not take long. As the Bobbseys walked into the hotel lobby a man rose from a chair and came up to them.

"Mr. Bobbsey?" he asked politely. "I am Miguel Delgado."

"How do you do?" Mr. Bobbsey replied, and introduced his family. He explained that Sr. Delgado was a lumberman and the man who was to take Mr. Bobbsey to see the cork trees. As the two men began to talk, the others went upstairs.

Later Mr. Bobbsey joined his family in their suite. He said that he would leave on his mission the next day and would be gone about a week.

"Sr. Delgado suggested that you might like to move to a small hotel he knows. It is run by an Englishwoman, Mrs. Watson, and is very old and interesting. In the sixteenth century the building was used as a convent."

"It sounds fascinating!" Nan declared.

"What's the name of the hotel?" Mrs. Bobbsey asked.

"It's called Pensão Inglesa, which could be translated as English Boarding House. It is on the Rua das Janelas Verdes, the Street of the Green Windows."

"What a pretty name!" said Flossie. "Are all the windows on the street green?"

"Perhaps they were once," her father replied, "but I don't imagine they are now."

Mrs. Bobbsey and the children moved the next morning. When the car stopped in front of the address given them, they saw only the old stone wall with an iron gate. Inside they found wide stone steps bordered with large pots of flowers.

"The hotel is built on the side of a hill!" Bert said, picking up two suitcases and starting to climb.

Just then two young men in green vests and black trousers came running down the steps. With many smiles they took charge of the luggage and motioned the Bobbseys to follow them.

At the top of the first flight they came to a small courtyard. To one side there appeared to be the basement of the hotel. A man was sawing wood in it.

The next flight of steps ended in a garden. Around three sides of this was the hotel. A wall extended along the fourth side. From it the Tagus River could be seen.

A tall, blond woman hurried out to greet her

guests. With her was a dark-haired girl of about sixteen whom Mrs. Watson introduced as her daughter Judy.

A little later, when Mrs. Bobbsey was unpacking, Bert asked if he and Nan might take the younger twins out to explore the city.

"If you will stay on the main streets, yes. But take this in case you get lost." Mrs. Bobbsey gave Bert an envelope with the address of the Pensão on it. "Show this to a taxi driver and he can bring you back."

The twins met Judy on their way out and asked her how to reach the center of the city.

"Go down to the next corner and take the trolley," she advised. "Say to the conductor, '*O Rossio*' and he will see that you get off at the central square."

The four children reached the corner just as a rickety little trolley car came along. They climbed aboard and found seats together. Nan looked at Bert and smiled. "Do you have the same idea I do?" she asked.

"If it's to ask in antique shops for the strange man who was at the quinta," he said, "I do!"

"That's it!" Nan declared.

The children peered from the windows of the car as it rattled up and down the hilly streets. Finally it came to a level area where there were many shops.

"We must be getting near *O Rossio*," Nan said and looked inquiringly at the conductor. But he smiled and shook his head.

Freddie and Flossie had their noses pressed against the glass. Suddenly Flossie grabbed her twin and pointed to the sidewalk. "Look!" she cried.

A short, fat, black-haired man was about to cross the street. As they watched he took something from his pocket and popped it into his mouth.

"It's candy!" Freddie exclaimed. "He's the fat man who likes candy that we're looking for!"

He jumped up and ran to the back of the car. The trolley stopped at the corner and Freddie hopped off.

"Freddie!" Bert called. But the little boy paid no attention. He was already halfway across the street. Quickly Bert, Nan and Flossie left the trolley and caught up to Freddie.

"You stay with us," Bert cautioned.

When the twins reached the opposite sidewalk, they saw the fat man turn down a side street. The children hurried after him. Finally, after several blocks, the Bobbseys saw him enter a tall, gray structure which stood in the middle of the street.

"Hurry!" Flossie urged. "We can catch him now!"

As they neared it they could see through long windows cables stretching upward from a car.

"Why, it's an elevator!" Bert exclaimed. "Right out in the middle of the street!"

The Bobbseys dashed forward when they saw several people, including the fat man, step into the elevator. Bert was just about to enter when he heard a man call from a little window near the entrance.

"I think we have to buy tickets," Nan said.

By the time Bert had paid the small charge, the elevator had started upward. Fuming, the children waited until it came down again, then hurried aboard. Once again it rose, leaving the busy streets of downtown Lisbon below it.

When the car finally stopped and the door slid open, the twins were amazed. They found themselves on a narrow street.

"This is great," said Bert. "You don't have to walk uphill to get to the high streets."

The fat man was not in sight.

"There's a park," Nan remarked, gazing to the left where the street opened into a broad, sunlit expanse of green grass and shade trees.

"Maybe that's where the man went," Freddie declared. "Let's see!" The twins raced down the street.

The park was actually the center of a small square surrounded by ancient houses. A few

"Did you take our green rooster?" Freddie asked

benches stood under the tall trees. At one side under a brightly striped awning was a refreshment stand.

"There he is!" Flossie cried, pointing to the attendant behind the little counter.

The fat man now had a big white apron tied around his waist and was busy selling ice cream cones to a group of children.

"What shall we do?" Nan asked uncertainly.

"Ask him about the green rooster!" Freddie declared. He ran toward the stand.

By the time the others came up, Freddie was saying to the man, "Did you take our green rooster?"

The Portuguese looked puzzled, then shrugged and raised his hands to indicate he did not understand.

"He doesn't speak English, Freddie," Bert said. "Let me try."

He turned to the man and said, *"Galo verde?"*

The ice cream man looked at the boy in bewilderment. The next instant he burst into laughter. *"Galo verde, não, não!"*

"I'm sure he isn't the thief," Nan declared. "He seems so nice and jolly. Let's buy some ice cream and then go back down to the city."

Bert pulled some coins from his pocket and motioned to the ice cream. The vendor gave a huge smile.

"Ah, *sim, sim,*" he cried and ladled out generous portions for each of the twins.

The children licked the cones as they made their way back to the elevator. When they were down in the busy section of Lisbon once more, Nan suggested, "Let's go to that street with the trolley tracks. There were lots of nice-looking shops along it."

"Okay," Bert agreed. "We can split up, and cover more places that way. Flossie and I will take one side of the street, and you and Freddie ask in the shops on the other side."

Reaching the bustling shopping area, the children separated. "We'll meet at the end," Bert directed. "That's probably *O Rossio,* or the main square."

Freddie and Nan made their way to the other side and began to walk along, peering into the display windows as they went.

"This looks like an antique shop," Nan said a few minutes later. She stopped in front of a small store. The window was filled with clocks of all kinds, metal, wood, and porcelain.

Nan and Freddie pushed open the door and went in. A short, thin man with gray hair stood behind a counter.

"*Bom dia,* good morning, *senhorita,*" he said to Nan with a smile. "May I help you?"

Nan was relieved to learn that the man spoke

English. She described the stranger who had visited Mr. Machado's quinta and asked if the shopkeeper knew such a person.

"I am sorry, senhorita," he said. "I do not recognize this man. There are many antique shops in Lisbon. Perhaps you will find him in one of those."

Nan and Freddie thanked the shopkeeper and continued their walk. On the other side of the street Bert and Flossie were asking about the fat man in another shop.

"That sounds like my cousin," the owner said.

"Does your cousin eat a lot of candy?" Flossie piped up.

The shop owner looked proud. "No, my cousin has not eaten a piece of candy for six months. He is trying to lose his fat!"

"I guess he's not the one we're looking for then," Bert said in a discouraged tone.

Nan and Freddie by now had reached the shop on the corner of *O Rossio*. "This is the last one." Nan sighed. "We haven't had any luck so far."

Again the children described the suspect. This shop owner, who was an energetic-looking man in a neat black suit, smiled at Nan and Freddie.

"That is a very good description," he said. "The man you seek must be Manuel Silva!"

CHAPTER VI

THE CLUE IN THE NOTE

"YOU know the man we're looking for?"

"Oh yes. Manuel works part time for me."

"Oh boy!" Freddie piped up. "May we see him?"

"He is not here. He has not been here for several days."

"Do you know where he lives? Perhaps we can go to his home," Nan persisted.

The shop owner told the children that Manuel had recently moved to a house on the Rua das Janelos Verdes, but that he did not know the number.

"We live on that street," Freddie declared. "We'll find him."

Outside the shop Nan and Freddie met Bert and Flossie and reported their success. "The shop owner says he is sure our fat, candy-eating man is Manuel Silva," Nan said. "Now, if we can only find him!"

The children had walked into the large square known as *O Rossio* while they were talking. They stopped to admire it. Trolley cars, taxis, and private automobiles sped around the huge square. At the edge of the broad sidewalks, crowds of people sat at tables sipping coffee and brightly colored fruit drinks.

"Look!" Flossie cried in surprise. "The pavement is made of little black and white stones."

"And they're in a design," Nan added, pointing out the swirling pattern of the mosaic.

Bert hailed a taxi. "We'd better get back to lunch," he said. "Mother will be waiting for us."

When they climbed the steps to the hotel level a few minutes later, the children peered in at the basement carpentry shop. The man looked up from his work and gave them a friendly smile.

"Let's go down and talk to him after lunch," Bert proposed. "Maybe he knows Manuel Silva."

When the meal was over, Mrs. Bobbsey took a book out into the garden. The twins ran down the steps to the old basement.

The cabinetmaker greeted them cordially. "Come in," he urged. "I will show you my workroom."

The children walked through the arched doorway into a dim room. It seemed to stretch far into the distance through a series of arches. The vaulted ceiling was high above them.

"You speak English!" Nan observed with pleasure.

The cabinetmaker, who was a small man with glasses, explained that he had learned English when he was a young man. There were many English guests at the Pensão, and he enjoyed talking to them.

"My name is Carlos Pinto," he said, "and I make furniture."

There were several long wooden workbenches near the door and the one window.

"We're the Bobbsey twins," Bert told him and introduced his sisters and brother.

"Your place looks sort of spooky," Flossie remarked with a little shiver.

"It used to be part of the old convent four hundred years ago," Carlos said as he led them through the many archways. They were lighted by several bulbs hanging from the high ceiling. Pieces of wood were stacked along one side while against the other were many unfinished chairs and tables.

"There is a mystery about this place," Carlos said with a smile.

"A mystery!" the twins chorused. "Tell us!"

"The story is that when this building was

used as a convent, there was a secret underground passage which ran out from this basement to the street. Now no one knows where it started or where it came out."

Freddie jumped up and down in excitement. "Let's look for the secret tunnel!" he cried.

Good-naturedly, Carlos went back to his work while the children examined the walls and floor of the workshop. Suddenly Freddie gave a triumphant cry.

"Here's something!" he called from the dim depths of the long room.

The other children ran to him. Freddie bent over and pulled at a large stone in the floor. It was loose! Bert dashed to one of the workbenches and brought back a crowbar.

Nan and Flossie watched breathlessly as the boys worked to raise the stone. Finally, with a great heave, they pried it up. They all bent forward eagerly.

There was nothing but dirt under the stone!

Disappointed, the children replaced the stone and went up front to talk to Carlos. Bert asked if the cabinetmaker knew a Manuel Silva.

"Yes, I do," Carlos admitted. "But I don't like him much."

Carlos said that Manuel sometimes bought pieces of furniture from him. "He always buys copies of antiques," the cabinetmaker went on. "I suspect that he sells them to others as real antiques."

Before Bert or Nan could ask another question Freddie blurted out, "Do you know anything about a green rooster?"

Carlos laughed. "I don't remember any special green rooster," he said, "but roosters are very popular in Portugal and are used in decorations of all kinds."

"Then," said Nan, "Mr. Machado's green

rooster could be just a decoration on almost anything."

Noticing Carlos's bewildered look, Bert explained about the missing gift and Manuel's possible connection with it.

"*Galo verde*," Carlos repeated in a puzzled tone. Then his face brightened. "I knew that reminded me of something! The note Manuel dropped yesterday when he was here! I kept it to give back to him."

Carlos opened a drawer in his workbench and took out a slip of paper. He handed it to Bert. Written in pencil were the Portuguese words:

Galo verde-Nazaré-Pedro-sábado.

"What does it all mean?" Bert asked.

"Green rooster, Nazaré—that's a fishing village up north of here—Pedro, Saturday."

"A clue!" Nan cried. "It must mean that Manuel is going to Nazaré on Saturday to see Pedro about a green rooster!"

The twins were jubilant. If they could only find Manuel and learn more about his visit to Nazaré.

"Do you know which house Manuel lives in?" Bert asked.

"Yes." Carlos led the Bobbseys out to the courtyard and over to the wall above the street. He pointed to a tall building painted pale green about halfway up the block.

"Manuel lives in that house," he said.

The four children said good-by to Carlos, ran down the steps and onto the sidewalk. A few minutes later Bert knocked on the door of the green building. There was no answer.

"Maybe it's sort of an apartment house," Nan suggested, "and we're supposed to walk in."

Bert turned the knob and the door opened. The other children followed him into a narrow hallway. A steep staircase led upward. Four doors opened into the hallway and on each was a white card with a name printed on it.

Bert and Nan looked at the cards, but there was no Manuel Silva. "Let's go upstairs. He must live on one of the other floors," Bert said.

"Oh! Do you think we should?" Flossie shuddered. "It's sort of scary in here!"

"I think it's all right, honey," Nan assured her little sister. "Take my hand."

The twins walked up to the second and third floors and read the names on the doors. None was Manuel Silva.

Climbing the stairs between the third and fourth floors, Freddie suddenly clutched Bert. "Someone is coming up behind us!" he whispered.

The children stopped to listen. *Clump! Clump!* The heavy footsteps drew nearer. They waited, holding their breath.

When the footsteps reached the hall beneath them, Bert leaned over the banister and peered down. A plump woman with black hair and eyes looked up at him inquiringly.

"We're looking for Manuel Silva," Bert told her.

The woman shook her head indicating that she did not understand. "Manuel Silva?" Bert repeated slowly.

The woman nodded and walked up the stairs past the children. Motioning them to follow, she went to one of the doors on the fourth floor and knocked.

"Manuel!" she called. No reply. The woman knocked again. Still there was no answer. She shrugged and waved the children down the stairs ahead of her.

"At least we know where he lives, even if we didn't find him," Nan remarked as they walked toward the pensão.

"Maybe Mother will drive us to Nazaré tomorrow," Bert said. "That note Manuel dropped mentioned Saturday and Nazaré, and tomorrow's Saturday."

"Let's ask her," Flossie urged, running up the stone steps to the garden.

Mrs. Bobbsey smiled when the twins suggested the trip. "I'll see what Mrs. Watson says about it," she promised.

Before the children went to bed that night, their mother told them they would go to the fishing village the next day.

"Mrs. Watson thinks Nazaré is one of the most interesting places in Portugal," she said. "It's about seventy miles north of here on the Atlantic coast. She says that if we wish to stay overnight there is a very small but nice hotel."

Next morning, when the overnight bags were packed and they were ready to go, Bert had an idea. "We should phone the Magros police. Maybe they've caught the thief who took the things from Mr. Machado's quinta. The officer was going to call us, but he doesn't know we've moved."

Mrs. Bobbsey agreed, and Bert put in the call. The Magros police reported that they had had no success in finding the thief. Also, they had received reports of two more burglaries in the area.

Bert told his family and said, "I think if we can find Manuel Silva, we'll solve the mystery."

"Our cock-a-doodle-doo mystery!" Flossie reminded him with a giggle.

"Maybe we'll catch him today!" Freddie remarked hopefully.

A good highway led north from Lisbon. As they neared the fishing village Mrs. Bobbsey turned off the main road toward the ocean. A short time later they rounded a corner and Nazaré lay before them.

It was a small town at the foot of a high headland. The white and colored houses had red tile roofs and were built very close together. The streets were narrow, cobbled, and hilly.

"What a strange town!" Nan cried. "There's no one around!"

It was true. The streets were deserted. There were no children playing, and no peddlers' carts rumbled over the stones.

Mrs. Bobbsey drove to the end of the street and turned right along the shore. The twins exclaimed in surprise. The wide, sandy beach was crowded with people!

"Something terrible must have happened!" Nan cried out.

CHAPTER VII

TWO PEDROS!

"MOTHER," Nan urged, "let's ask someone what the trouble is!"

Mrs. Bobbsey stopped the car in front of one of the shops which lined the waterfront street. Bert leaned out the window and called to a man lounging in a doorway.

"What's the matter? Why are all the people on the beach?"

The man seemed surprised at the question. In halting English he replied, "Everyone wait for fishing boats."

The Bobbseys looked again at the beach. Now they noticed that the crowd was made up largely of women. They sat on the thick sand, their heads and shoulders wrapped in black shawls and their full skirts spread around them. Little girls dressed in the same fashion and boys in dunga-

rees and plaid shirts played in the sand or in the
rowboats which were drawn up on the beach.

Nan sighed in relief. "Thank goodness, nothing's wrong!"

Freddie turned back to the man. "Do you
know Pedro?" he asked.

The man laughed heartily. "I know many
Pedros. They're all out fishing." With that he
walked into the shop. Next to it was a store with
many bright aprons, skirts, and handbags in the
window. In front of them stood a doll dressed in
peasant costume. A girl who appeared to be a
little older than Flossie was standing by the
window staring in admiration at the doll.

"I'm going to ask her if she knows Pedro,"
Flossie announced.

She hopped from the car and ran toward the
little Portuguese girl. The child turned around.
Her brown hair was parted in the middle and
hung down her back in two long braids. Tiny
golden earrings gleamed in her ears.

Nan and the boys hurried to join Flossie.

"This is Anna," Flossie told them, "and she
wears a lot of petticoats!" Flossie pointed to the
little girl's full plaid skirt.

Anna giggled. With one hand she raised her
skirt slightly to reveal layer after layer of bright-
colored cotton. Then she held up seven fingers.
"Sete!" she said.

"And she's going to take us to see Pedro!" Flossie announced, after Nan had admired the petticoats.

"That's neat!" said Freddie. "Let's go!"

Anna beckoned the twins to follow her. Nan hurried to the car and told her mother where they were going.

"All right," said Mrs. Bobbsey, "but don't go far. I'll wait here for you."

Anna hurried ahead, her full skirt swishing about her bare brown legs. A minute later Anna turned up a narrow street.

"If this Pedro is the one in the note," said Bert, "I wonder if we'll find Manuel with him."

"And the green rooster!" Flossie reminded him as they hastened along past the tall, narrow houses.

Anna stopped at a yellow stucco house and knocked on the door. It was opened by a smiling young woman.

Anna spoke to her in Portuguese and the Bobbseys heard the word Pedro. The woman grinned broadly and stepped aside to let the children enter the house. Anna beckoned the Bobbseys and tiptoed into a room to the right of the door.

A tiny baby lay asleep in a wooden crib in one corner of the room. "Pedro!" Anna announced.

Flossie ran over and peered into the crib. "He's 'dorable!" she cried. Then she said to Anna, who was watching her intently, "But I don't think this is the right Pedro!"

When Anna saw Nan and the boys shaking their heads also, she looked sad. But in a few seconds her face brightened. She motioned the twins toward the door. They waved good-by to the baby's mother and went out.

This time Anna led them back to the waterfront and looked up and down the street. She ran a short distance ahead, then stopped beside a little burro. It was standing sleepily before a bakery.

Anna pointed at the little animal. "Pedro?"

The Bobbseys patted him and Nan said, "He's sweet. But not the Pedro we want."

This time Anna's dark eyes filled with tears. She was not giving up, however, and motioned them to follow her to the beach.

The twins looked around with interest. The women sat in large groups, knitting and talking. Some men were busy mending fishing nets or working on the boats high up on the sand. The younger children stayed near the women. Many of the older ones either watched or helped the men.

"Whole families must come here for the day," Nan observed.

"Look at the funny hats!" Flossie exclaimed.

The men wore what looked like long black wool stocking caps with a tassel on the end. Their shirts or trousers, and sometimes both, were made of plaid material. Everyone on the beach was barefoot.

Anna ran up to a man in a pink-and-white shirt who was repairing a net near one of the boats. She spoke pleadingly to him in Portuguese. The twins stood by curiously.

The man turned to them with a smile. "My daughter Anna tells me you are looking for someone," he said in English. "Perhaps I can help you. I am José and this is my son Paulo." He motioned to a good-looking boy in his early teens working on the boat.

"I'm glad you speak English," Bert remarked. "I guess we couldn't make Anna understand exactly what we were asking."

José explained that both he and his son spoke English. "I lived in Gloucester, Massachusetts, until I came back to Portugal and married. There are almost as many Portuguese people in Gloucester as there are in Nazaré," he said with a chuckle.

"Why is that?" asked Bert.

"Gloucester too is a great fishing port, and a great many Portuguese are fishermen," was the reply.

"Who is it you are looking for?" Paulo asked.

Bert and Nan told him about their search for the green rooster and the note which Manuel Silva had dropped in the cabinetmaker's shop. "So you see, we're trying to find a man named Pedro who may have something to do with our green rooster," Nan concluded.

Paulo looked at his father. "Do you think it could be Pedro Kanos, who has the shop on the waterfront?"

José nodded. "Perhaps. Pedro has been acting very strange lately. He has suddenly become rich and has bought a motor bike. I am told he is away from Nazaré for several days each week."

"Can you tell us where his shop is?" Nan asked. "We'd like to talk to him."

"It is on the corner across from my home," José replied. "He lives above the shop."

Now Anna's father pointed to a little iron stove on the sand in the lee of his boat. "My wife has gone up the coast to visit her mother, so I am about to cook our dinner. We would be honored to have you join us."

"Oh, yes! Nan, please let's!" Flossie begged. "We can look for Pedro later. I'm hungry!"

"Me too!" Freddie said eagerly.

Nan explained that their mother was waiting in the car. "Ask her to come down," José insisted.

Nan and Flossie ran up to the street to bring Mrs. Bobbsey. When the three returned José was frying sardines in a huge skillet. Then, after Mrs. Bobbsey had been introduced, he added sliced onions and tomatoes to the fish.

"That smells yummy!" Nan observed as she bent to empty some sand from her shoes.

"You should take off your shoes and socks," Paulo advised. "No one in Nazaré wears them!"

The children looked inquiringly at their mother. She nodded consent.

"This feels great!" Freddie said as he wiggled his toes in the soft, cool sand.

Anna produced plates and forks from a large basket. Paulo sliced a long loaf of bread and the dinner was ready. They all sat down.

"I've never tasted anything so good!" Mrs. Bobbsey remarked after she had finished the last bit of food on her plate. "Tell me, why are those oxen on the beach?" She nodded toward a pair of sleek, brown animals near the water's edge.

"They pull up the boats when the fishermen return," José replied.

He went on to explain that since the beach was on the open Atlantic and there was no shelter where the boats could be anchored, they had to be hauled up onto the sand when not in use.

"Sometimes the men do this work, but if a

José was frying sardines in a huge skillet

fisherman can afford it, he buys a pair of oxen."
José smiled. "Sometimes nowadays the fishermen buy a tractor together to take the place of oxen!"

"Which do you have?" Freddie asked.

"We still use oxen," Paulo answered as his father resumed working on the nets.

Nan and Flossie helped Anna scour the plates with sand and put them back into the basket.

A few minutes later the Bobbseys noticed a spurt of activity farther down the beach. "Come on!" Paulo called. "The oxen are going to pull in a boat now. You can see how it's done."

The four twins, with Paulo and Anna, ran toward a group of men. By the time the children reached the scene, the oxen had been harnessed to the boat.

The brightly painted craft had an upturned prow and stern. The seats were wide enough for four men to sit at each oar position. On one side of the prow was a drawing of a huge eye.

"What's that for?" Freddie asked in surprise.

"That's the eye that finds the fish!" Paulo grinned. "It's an old custom to paint one on the boat."

Flossie had been staring at the other side of the prow. Now she cried, "A green rooster! See, it's a green rooster!"

All the Bobbseys looked at the painting. It

showed a rooster with an arched tail and high red comb. The body of the bird was green.

"The man who owns the boat painted the rooster on it so everyone would know it is Portuguese!" Paulo explained.

"Oh!" Freddie sounded disappointed. "I thought maybe it was *our* green rooster."

By this time the boat had been rowed to the edge of the sand. A man urged the oxen forward. The ropes which led from the animals to the boat grew taut. The oxen strained, and the craft began to move up onto the beach.

Suddenly Freddie noticed a little girl about two years old get up from the sand and toddle toward the oxen. The next instant she was directly in the path of the animals!

Freddie dashed over and grabbed the child's arm. He pulled her away just as the oxen put on an extra burst of speed!

"Oh! Oh! *Obrigado! Obrigado!*" A woman wearing a black shawl dashed up to Freddie and threw her arms around the boy. She covered his face with kisses.

Freddie turned red and tried to squirm from the woman's grasp. At that moment a bell clanged noisily in the distance. The woman released Freddie so fast he almost fell. She began to run toward a nearby boat!

CHAPTER VIII

A SLIPPERY CATCH

FREDDIE looked around him, bewildered. The sound of the bell had turned the beach into a beehive of activity. Men were heading for the boats, women were dragging out the nets. Children, chattering excitedly, had lined up at the edge of the water.

"What happened?" Freddie asked Paulo.

The Portuguese boy pointed to the high bluff at the north end of the beach. "A man is stationed up there to watch," he explained. "When he spots a shoal of fish in the ocean, he rings the bell. Then the men race to take the boats out."

"I want to go in a fishing boat!" Freddie declared.

Paulo started back up the beach. "Perhaps my father will take you out in his boat if your mother allows. I must help him."

Freddie and Flossie dashed ahead to where

their mother was seated on the sand. "May we go out with José to catch the fish?" Freddie asked breathlessly.

Mrs. Bobbsey looked surprised. "Is that what all the excitement is about?"

Bert and Nan hurried up and explained to her about the sighting of the fish. "The boats are ready to go out after them," Bert added. "Paulo thinks his father will take Freddie and Flossie along if you'll let them go."

"Please, Mommy, say yes!" Flossie begged.

"Don't you and Nan want to go?" Mrs. Bobbsey said. Bert looked at his twin, who said, "I think I'd rather try to find Pedro and Manuel."

"So would I," Bert agreed.

Now José himself walked over. "There is really no danger in this short a run," he assured Mrs. Bobbsey. "The young ones would like to go?"

"Oh, yes!" chorused the small twins.

"Very well," said Mrs. Bobbsey, "but you both must do just what José and Paulo tell you."

Freddie and Flossie nodded happily and ran off to join Paulo at the fishing boat. Meanwhile, José gave Bert and Nan directions for finding Pedro Kanos's shop, and the older twins started toward the street. Anna sat down beside Mrs. Bobbsey and began to untangle a snarled fishing line.

A few minutes later José lifted Freddie and Flossie into the boat, then climbed aboard. He took his place at the oars with one twin on either side of him. Paulo sat behind. Finally several other men pushed the boat out into the water. They quickly jumped aboard and manned the oars. In another minute the boat was cleaving through the breakers.

"Ooh! This is fun!" Flossie gasped as the fresh wind whipped her hair.

Paulo whispered to Freddie, "We are paying out the net. When we get to the school of fish we turn and the fish are scooped up into the net. Then we pull it in and dump the fish in the stern of the boat."

Freddie's eyes sparkled with excitement at the prospect of seeing so many fish. The steady rowing of the oarsmen continued to speed the boat over the water.

Suddenly, at a signal from José, they turned the craft parallel to the shore. Freddie and Flossie peered over the side into the water. Four of the men began to drag in the net. The twins could see that it was full of floundering, silvery fish! Nearer and nearer to the side of the boat the heavy net came.

Soon the men began to dump the fish into the stern. Freddie and Flossie, with arms folded, watched intently. The net was almost empty when a large fish flipped into the air and landed in Freddie's arms! The little boy was so surprised that he fell backward.

"Don't lose him, Freddie!" Flossie shrieked.

She leaned forward and tried to grasp the slippery fish. It slithered to the bottom of the boat, where it flopped around, splashing water over the twins.

Paulo reached down and grabbed the fish by the gills. He quickly tossed it into the stern, then grinned at the children. "Your mother will be surprised to see you!" he said.

Freddie and Flossie looked at each other and began to laugh. Not only were they both very wet, but a few scales from the struggling fish had landed in Flossie's curls.

While the younger twins were having a big laugh over this, Bert and Nan had been busy. They had finally found Pedro's shop.

When Bert and Nan entered, a bell tinkled. They gazed around. The place was full of odds and ends. There were several pieces of old furniture, some pottery, and straw baskets of various shapes and sizes. A few seconds later, a tall, thin man came in from a room at the back.

"Are you Pedro Kanos?" Bert asked. The man nodded.

"We're looking for a person named Manuel Silva," Bert continued. "Do you know him?"

A large fish landed in Freddie's arms

Pedro looked suspiciously at Bert, then shook his head.

"Does a green rooster mean anything to you?" Bert asked.

Pedro said nothing, but walked to the other side of the room and indicated some pottery roosters on a shelf. At this moment a sound at the doorway to the back room made Nan look in that direction. A short, very fat man stood there obviously listening to every word. As soon as he saw Nan watching him, he turned into the room again.

"Bert!" Nan whispered. "I think Manuel Silva is here—I just saw him in the doorway!"

While Pedro was looking at the rooster, Bert edged over to the back room and peered inside. He was just in time to see a fat man hurrying out a rear door.

"Come on, Nan!" Bert cried. He and his twin ran through the room and outside.

The fat man was running. He was surprisingly fast for one so heavy. He dashed around the corner into the waterfront street, with Bert and Nan not far behind.

The street, instead of being empty as it had been when the Bobbseys had driven into town, was now crowded with people. Many were pushing trucks, carts, and wheelbarrows filled with fish. All were going in one direction.

"There must be a fish market up ahead," Bert gasped as he and Nan raced along.

The fat man dodged in and out among the carts until finally Bert and Nan lost sight of him completely. They ran on for another block, but the man had disappeared.

"Let's go back and see Pedro again," Nan proposed. "Maybe we can find out if that fat man is the Manuel Silva we're looking for."

"Okay. But I don't think he'll tell us."

When Bert and Nan entered the shop, Pedro came to meet them. Before they could question him, he said, "I have been thinking about what you asked me. I suggest you take the cable railroad to the bluff at the upper end of town. If you inquire at the first house on your right as you get off, you may find the person you seek."

"I guess that man we chased wasn't Manuel Silva?" Nan said, a little embarrassed.

Pedro laughed. "Oh no, he is my cousin from Sintra. He just stopped in to see me. You must have scared him away!"

"We're sorry," said Bert. "We'll try the house on the bluff."

The two children hurried back to the beach to tell their mother what had happened and to ask if they might take the cable car ride. She had just given her consent when José's boat came toward the shore.

At a signal the oxen were harnessed to it and slowly they pulled the craft up onto the sand. Freddie and Flossie jumped out and ran to their family.

"Goodness!" exclaimed Mrs. Bobbsey. "What in the world happened to you?"

"Freddie caught a floppy fish in his arms!" Flossie cried, her blue eyes shining impishly.

One of the fishermen's wives had been watching the Bobbseys. She went over to José and said a few words.

He came to speak to Mrs. Bobbsey. "My friend says she has children's clothes to fit Freddie and Flossie. They're in the cabin of her husband's boat. She will be glad to lend them to you until theirs are dry." José pointed to a large boat nearby on the beach.

Mrs. Bobbsey smiled her thanks and, with Freddie and Flossie, followed the woman to the boat. In a short while they were back.

"You look terrific!" Nan exclaimed when she saw the small twins.

Flossie wore a white blouse and a long full skirt of black and white stripes. It was split in front to show seven pleated petticoats.

Freddie's blue and tan plaid shirt was tucked into corduroy trousers. On his head was a little black cap with the peak in back.

"Please tell your friend we'll return the

clothes in the morning," Mrs. Bobbsey said to José.

Flossie clapped her hands. "Goody!" she cried. "We're going to stay here overnight!"

José directed Mrs. Bobbsey to the small hotel which Mrs. Watson in Lisbon had recommended. Two rooms were available, so Bert and Freddie carried up the bags.

"Nan and I are going to the upper town to see if we can find out something about Manuel," Bert told the younger twins. "Do you two want to come?"

"Yes!" Freddie accepted at once.

But Flossie shook her head. "I have some shopping to do," she said importantly.

Nan smiled. "You take Freddie, Bert," she suggested. "I'd like to go shopping too."

After the boys had left, Flossie told her mother and Nan an idea which had occurred to her. "I'd like to give Anna that dolly she was looking at when we first saw her. I remember where the shop is."

"That's a very nice idea, honey," Mrs. Bobbsey agreed. "We'll go right now."

In the meantime Bert and Freddie were riding up the slope in the little cable car. Bert told his brother about his and Nan's experience in Pedro's shop.

"He must not be the right Pedro if he didn't

know anything about Manuel or the green rooster," Freddie commented.

"I wonder," said Bert. "Why did that man run away? Anyhow, maybe we can find a clue up here."

The car came to a jerky halt, and the boys got off. "That must be the house over there." Bert indicated a one-story building of faded pink stucco.

The two boys walked over to the shabby-looking house and Bert knocked on the door. It was immediately opened by an elderly man. He was unshaven and his coarse gray hair stood up in spikes all over his head.

"Pedro Kanos sent us," Bert began. He got no further. The man began to shout and wave his arms. Bert and Freddie backed away.

As the man continued to yell at the children, doors opened along the street and people ran out to see what was causing the commotion. In a few minutes a crowd had gathered.

"Oh, Bert! What are we going to do?" Freddie asked in alarm.

Before Bert could reply a policeman pushed his way up to the boys. He said a few words in Portuguese and put his hands on their shoulders.

"I think we're being arrested!" Bert cried out.

CHAPTER IX

A BEACH CHASE

THE policeman's hands dropped from the boys' shoulders. "I am sorry. You are Americans. I thought you were a couple of the naughty boys who come here to tease this man."

The officer smiled and put one hand on Freddie's head. "You are dressed like our fishermen's sons," he said, "but your yellow hair did puzzle me. Most Portuguese people have dark hair."

By this time the elderly man had slammed his door shut, still muttering. The crowd, seeing that the excitement was over, wandered away.

"We didn't mean to make any trouble," Bert apologized. "We were looking for a man named Manuel Silva. Do you know him?"

"Is there a green rooster around here?" Freddie asked at the same time.

The policeman laughed. "I haven't seen one if

there is!" he replied. "And I don't know a Manuel Silva. Why are you looking for him?"

Bert told him about the theft of the gift which had something to do with a green rooster and their suspicion that Manuel Silva was the thief. "We were sent here to find out about him."

"Who sent you?" the officer inquired.

"Pedro Kanos."

"I cannot understand why. Pedro must know that the man who lives in this house never allows anyone to set foot on his property!"

The policeman walked with the two boys to the cable car. "Perhaps you misunderstood Pedro," he said as they climbed aboard. "He may have meant some other house."

The car started its downhill journey, and the boys waved good-by to their new friend.

"There's something queer about this," Bert told Freddie. "I didn't misunderstand Pedro."

"Maybe he wanted you and Nan to go away from his shop, so he sent you up there. He knew that man was mean and he meant to scare you!"

Later when the boys told their story, Nan and Flossie agreed with Freddie. "I'm sure Pedro knows something about the green rooster!" Nan declared.

"Anna came to see us while you were gone," Flossie told Bert and Freddie. "We're invited to her house to supper."

"Didn't José say Pedro's shop was just across the side street from his house?" Bert asked.

"Yes," Nan replied. "Why?"

"Well, I have an idea. We can keep a watch on Pedro from the window of José's house. I have a feeling he may try to meet Manuel tonight!"

The children agreed that it should be possible to take turns watching Pedro's place while they were at supper.

Mrs. Bobbsey and the twins found José's home to be on the ground floor of an old building. The front room had one window facing the beach and a second that looked out onto the side street. This seemed to be both the living and dining room. There was a tiny kitchen at one side and back of these were two small bedrooms.

Anna's dark eyes grew round with astonishment when Flossie held out the doll to her.

"This is for you," Flossie said. "I hope you like her."

The little Portuguese girl took the doll and held it to her tightly. She was speechless with happiness.

"Say thank you," her father urged, smiling.

Anna blushed and looked at the floor. "Sank you," she said softly.

Paulo said with a grin, "That was kind of you." He motioned the Bobbseys to take seats at the table in the center of the room. "I hope you like soup. When my mother goes away she always makes a large pot of soup and we have it for supper every evening until she comes home!"

"It looks delicious," said Mrs. Bobbsey.

She watched with interest as Paulo ladled out large bowls for everyone. It was a thick soup, full of tender pieces of fish, potatoes and onions.

"It's yummy," Flossie declared after tasting her first spoonful. Then she did as Anna was doing and broke pieces of crusty bread into the soup.

The twins were so busy enjoying the soup that they almost forgot what they had planned to do.

Suddenly Freddie put down his spoon. "Who's watching for Pedro?" he asked.

Seeing the puzzled expressions on the faces of José and Paulo, Bert explained what had happened that afternoon and told about his idea.

Bert's seat faced the side window. "I can see the shop entrance from here," he assured Freddie.

They had just finished their dessert of soft, white cheese when Bert jumped up from his chair. "There goes Pedro now!" he exclaimed.

The twins rushed to the window. Pedro was locking the door of his shop. He wore rough-looking dark clothes and the black stocking cap of the Nazaré fishermen.

"Who wants to trail him with me?" Bert asked.

Everyone wished to go, but Mrs. Bobbsey persuaded Freddie and Flossie to stay with her. Paulo volunteered to accompany Bert and Nan.

By the time the three had left the house, Pedro had crossed the street and jumped over the low wall onto the sand. He set off up the beach at a brisk pace. The children ran across the road and made their way down to the waterfront.

The sun had dropped below the horizon some time before and it was growing dark. The many boats which had been pulled up onto the beach were dark masses on the sand.

"It's going to be hard to follow Pedro in the dark," Paulo cautioned. "Watch out for all the things on the sand."

The boats were dark and deserted, but small iron stoves, nets, and boxes of fishing lines littered the beach.

"I have my flash." Bert pulled a pencil-slim flashlight from his pocket and shone it on the sand.

Paulo looked at it admiringly. "That is *bom,* good."

"Don't turn it on too often," Nan advised. "We don't want Pedro to know we're following him."

Bert snapped off the light and they went on. Pedro was only a dark shape hurrying along the beach. At times he would disappear. Then one of the children would catch sight of him once more against the lighter sky.

It was hard walking through the thick sand, and they stopped frequently to rest, then ran on again. Pedro kept up his steady pace.

"He's stopping!" Nan whispered finally, grabbing Bert's arm and halting him.

The three children watched as Pedro paused beside a boat and lighted a cigarette. A second later a short, broad form emerged from the shadow of the boat and joined him.

"If we're going to prove anything," said Nan, "we must get nearer and hear what they're saying!"

She began to run up the beach, dodging from one boat to the next. The two boys followed. Finally Nan reached the shadow of a boat next to the one where the men were standing. In the quiet night the voices of Pedro and the other man carried plainly to the listening children, but it was all in Portuguese.

Pedro was doing most of the talking. He addressed the other man as Manuel. In a bare whisper Paulo translated a little of it, then stopped. Nan poked Bert and when he looked up she nodded her head triumphantly. Bert grinned knowingly and held up two fingers in a V for Victory sign.

One word which Bert and Nan heard most frequently used sounded like *moynyoh*. What could it mean, they wondered. Neither dared ask Paulo for fear the men would hear them.

A wind had sprung up and it became harder to distinguish the men's conversation. Nan shivered

in her thin sweater. Then her nose began to tickle.

"I want to sneeze!" she thought desperately, "but I mustn't! Pedro would know we're here!"

But the sneeze would not be stopped. Nan tried to stifle the sound with her handkerchief, but it was no use.

Achoo! At the sound both men jumped. Pedro said a few quick words, then dashed off down the beach. Manuel's form faded into the shadows and disappeared. Bert immediately ran to the boat, but there was no sign of the fat man. He seemed to have melted into the night.

"Maybe we can catch Pedro!" Paulo called and took off after the man at top speed. Bert and Nan raced beside him.

"Something's stopped him!" Bert cried a minute later.

The tip of Pedro's stocking cap had caught on the rough end of an oar which protruded from one of the boats. He hesitated a moment, then evidently decided it was not worth the risk to try disentangling it. Pedro went on, leaving the cap dangling from the oar.

"Let him go!" Bert exclaimed when he reached the boat. "We can't catch him!" He plucked the long wool cap from the rough wood.

"Say!" he said in excitement. "There's something in the end of this cap."

"That's where fishermen keep their money," Paulo said.

Bert thrust his hand into the stocking cap and pulled out a small object. He flashed his light on the piece.

It was a tiny gold sailing ship!

CHAPTER X

THE GO-AROUND WHISTLE

"THAT looks very valuable!" Paulo exclaimed. "Where did Pedro get it?"

"I have a good idea," Bert said grimly. "Let's take it back to your house where we can see it better."

Bert put the little ship in his pocket, but hung the cap back on the oar. He thought, "Pedro may come back for it and then the police can catch him!"

The three children made their way to José's home. Mrs. Bobbsey and the younger twins were still there, talking to José and Anna. They looked up in surprise when Bert and Nan burst into the room.

"Did you catch Pedro?" Freddie asked immediately.

"No," Bert replied, "but we found something very suspicious." He put the gold filigree ship on the table.

"It's like the ones at the quinta!" Freddie cried. "Where did you get it?"

Nan, Bert, and Paulo told the story of their chase up the beach. "Then Pedro lost his cap and Bert found this tucked in the end of it," Nan finished the account.

"Do you think it is the one stolen from Mr. Machado's house?" Mrs. Bobbsey asked.

"We don't know. Remember, Tony showed us the maker's initials on the bottom of those at the quinta?" Nan remarked. "See if there are initials on this one, Bert."

Her twin turned the little ship over, and they all bent forward eagerly to see the bottom. The letters *L.V.* stood out plainly.

"It must be the stolen one!" Nan exclaimed. "And Manuel stole it and gave it to Pedro tonight!"

"Be careful, Nan," her mother warned. "You shouldn't accuse anyone of theft until you are sure."

"At least we ought to tell the police," Bert declared.

José and Mrs. Bobbsey agreed that this was the thing to do, so Paulo and the older twins hurried to police headquarters with their find. There the officer in charge took the little sailing ship, promising to turn it over to the Magros authorities.

"If the housekeeper can identify it, we will arrest Pedro," the policeman said. "I'll get him now and bring him in for questioning."

The officer and the three children walked back to Pedro's shop. When they reached it, Paulo pointed to a notice in Portuguese which had been tacked to the door.

"What does it say?" Nan asked.

"The shop will be closed for the summer," Paulo translated.

"So our bird has flown!" said the officer.

"Maybe," said Bert, "he'll come back to the beach and get his cap."

"Then we will catch him," the policeman said. "Pedro is not too clever!"

When the policeman had left, Bert remembered something. "What does *moynyoh* mean, Paulo? I heard that word several times while Pedro and Manuel were talking."

"*Moinho* is a mill," the Portuguese boy replied. "They were speaking very fast and I could not hear all they said. But they seemed to be planning to meet at a mill or hiding something at a mill. I am sorry I could not get it all."

"A mill," Bert mused. "I wonder which one they meant?"

Paulo had no suggestion. Freddie and Flossie were disappointed to learn that Pedro had escaped. As they said good night to José and Anna,

Freddie assured them that the Bobbseys would soon catch the man who had stolen the sailing ship.

Next morning Flossie and Freddie put on their own clothes which had been laundered overnight at the hotel. The borrowed costumes, also washed and ironed, were put into a bundle. After church Mrs. Bobbsey parked the car along the waterfront and followed the twins down to the sand. José, Paulo, and Anna were already there. They reported that Pedro's cap was gone.

"I wonder if the police caught him," Nan said.

Flossie took the bundle of clothes to the fisherman's wife. "Thank you very much," she said. "Freddie and I had fun being Portuguese."

José translated and the woman nodded happily.

"And I'd like you to have my flashlight," Bert said to Paulo, handing him the pencil flash. "Use it in case you chase anyone else on the beach at night!"

José, Paulo, and Anna stood on the sand waving as the Americans' car pulled away. After a stop for lunch, Mrs. Bobbsey and the twins reached the Pensão Inglesa late in the afternoon. Mrs. Watson and Judy welcomed them warmly.

"I have put your mail in your room," Mrs. Watson told them.

"Maybe there's a letter from Daddy!" Flossie cried, dashing up the stairs.

They did find a letter from him, and Mrs. Bobbsey read it aloud. He expected to be back in Lisbon the next Saturday and they would fly to the United States the day afterward.

"That's only a week from now!" Nan cried. "We *must* solve the mystery before we go home!"

"Here's something that may help us," Bert spoke up. He had been studying a post card addressed to him.

"What does the card say?" Freddie asked.

"It's from Tony and all he has written is: 'Clue in go-around whistle.' "

"Go-around whistle," Nan repeated. "What can that mean?"

"I don't know, but I'd like to go back to Magros and see Tony," Bert declared.

"Yes, please. May we, Mommy?" Flossie pleaded.

Mrs. Bobbsey laughingly agreed, so the next day the family started out again with their overnight bags. It was a bright sunny day and a brisk wind was blowing.

"If we could only find the missing second page of Mr. Machado's letter," Nan pointed out, "we would know what he meant by the green rooster."

"Maybe he forgot to put it in the envelope," Flossie suggested.

"Let's look around his house for it," proposed Freddie.

"We're getting near the quinta now," Mrs. Bobbsey said. "Shall we drive into Magros and get Tony?"

"Yes. We want to know what his clue is," Bert replied.

Mrs. Bobbsey slowed down as she drove past the Machado property and they all looked at the pink stucco house. It appeared deserted. Suddenly a low, whistling sound came to their ears. They looked at one another. Was this what Tony had meant by his message on the post card?

"But where is the whistling coming from?" Nan asked, puzzled. No one could answer her question.

As they drove on into Magros Bert asked his mother to stop at police headquarters. He ran in to ask if they had yet caught the thief. Officer Dias told him that he had received the little gold filigree sailing ship from the Nazaré police that morning and that Maria had identified it as the one taken from the quinta.

"But Pedro has not been picked up and we haven't found the thieves. There continue to be more burglaries," he said in a worried tone. "The Nazaré officer told me about how you overheard

Pedro Kanos and Manuel Silva talking, and we hope to catch them soon."

Bert wished the policeman luck and went out to the car. He told the others that the ship Pedro had in his cap was definitely the one stolen from Mr. Machado's house.

"Now if we can only find the green rooster," Nan said.

Maria and Tony were at home and were glad to go to the quinta with the Bobbseys. The children told Tony about the whistling sound they had heard as they passed the Machado estate.

"That's my clue!" Tony told them proudly. "I'll show you when we reach the quinta!"

At the estate Maria and Mrs. Bobbsey went into the house, but Tony beckoned the children to follow him. He led them up a little hill back of the house. An old windmill stood at the summit. It was round with a pointed top. The lower part was dirty white limestone. Split and ragged canvas covered the revolving arms.

As the children drew nearer, the whistling sound became louder. "Why, it's coming from the windmill!" Nan exclaimed in surprise.

Tony pointed out the stays connecting the poles which formed the arms. On them were fastened tiny clay pots. As the arms moved in the wind, the pots gave off the whistling sounds.

The whistling sound became louder

"You found a clue in here?" Bert asked.

Tony nodded proudly. He led the way into the mill. Inside it was dim and empty. "No more used," Tony explained. In halting English he told the twins that a few days before he had gone into the mill in search of stray sheep. He had been surprised to see a package there against one wall. The boy had thought perhaps it was the one which had been taken from the quinta.

"And was it?" Freddie interrupted.

Tony grinned. "I think I play detective like you. I look for address on package but none there. Then I send you card."

Bert and Nan looked at each other. "Mill," Nan said. "Could this be the mill Pedro and Manuel were talking about?"

"Paulo said they spoke of hiding something at a mill," Bert exclaimed. He turned back to Tony. "Where is the package now?"

Tony started over to the side, then stopped. "It's gone!" he cried. "Someone has taken it! I am not good detective!"

"Never mind. It's not your fault," Nan comforted him. "We have an idea who took it."

Tony listened with interest as Bert and Nan related the events at Nazaré. "So you see, it all ties in," Bert concluded.

The children went back to the house. Mrs.

Bobbsey showed them a letter which had just arrived for Mr. Machado.

"It's the one your father wrote about our coming to Portugal. His secretary sent it by ship instead of by air. That's the reason Mr. Machado didn't receive it before he left for Brazil."

Nan mentioned her idea of trying to find the second sheet of Mr. Machado's letter to her father. "Let's search the house for it," she said.

"Okay!" Freddie and Flossie began to run through the rooms, peering into corners and under furniture.

Nan wandered into a room which had evidently been Mr. Machado's library. The walls were lined with books, and a heavy carved desk stood in front of a window. As Nan looked around the room, something white caught her eye. She got down on her hands and knees and reached under the desk. A piece of paper was wedged between the floor boards.

Quickly Nan pulled it out. It was the missing second page!

"It must have blown off the desk without Mr. Machado's noticing," Nan thought. She read the foreign-looking writing, then called excitedly for the others to come.

When they ran into the room, she waved the paper in the air. "Now I know what the green rooster is!" she cried.

CHAPTER XI

THE MISSING ROOSTER

"THE green rooster!" Flossie echoed her sister. "What is it? Tell us quick!"

"It's a tile picture!"

"A picture of a green rooster?" Freddie asked. He sounded disappointed.

"Not exactly. You remember Mr. Machado wrote that he wanted Daddy to have something of his which was very old and valuable?"

The others nodded.

"Well, the description of it is on this page. It's an antique tile picture showing the Quinta do San Francisco as it was in the sixteenth century. It was made by a famous artist of that time."

"But where's the green rooster?" Flossie cried impatiently.

Nan went on to explain that the picture had a border of tiles showing different farm animals.

The tile in the lower right hand corner bore the artist's signature and the picture of a green rooster.

Turning back to the letter, Nan read the last lines on the page. " 'In Portugal it has always been known as the tile of the—' The page ends there."

"I see!" Bert exclaimed. "It fits the first two words on the last page Dad received—*galo verde!*"

"That's right!" said Nan. "Now we know what we're looking for—a tile picture of the quinta with a green rooster in the corner."

"But where is it?" Flossie wailed.

"Well," Bert went on, "we're fairly certain that Manuel Silva stole the gold sailing ship. He either gave or sold it to Pedro in Nazaré. If he also stole the tile picture, he may have taken that to Nazaré too."

"The note Carlos showed us mentioned the green rooster and Nazaré," Nan reminded Bert.

"Let's go back there!" Freddie jumped up and down.

Tony had been listening eagerly. Now he spoke up. "But package in windmill? Maybe that was picture."

"You could be right, Tony," Bert agreed. "I think we should make a search around here for that package."

"Would it be possible for us to stay here in the quinta overnight while the twins hunt for the picture?" Mrs. Bobbsey asked Tony.

The boy translated the question for his mother.

A happy smile spread over her face. *"Sim, sim,"* she cried and spoke in Portuguese to Tony.

He reported that his mother would be glad to make up beds for the Bobbseys. The china and silver had been packed for shipment to Brazil, but Maria could give them supper in the kitchen if they would not mind.

"My mother still keeps food here because we sometimes stay all night when we are working," Tony explained.

"That will be very nice," Mrs. Bobbsey agreed. "We have a picnic lunch with us and hope you and your mother will join us."

Bert ran out and brought in the picnic basket from the car, which was parked outside the front gate. "Where shall we eat?" he asked.

"By the fountain!" Flossie urged.

The others thought this was a good idea, so Maria and Tony brought a wrought iron table and chairs and set them in the middle of the patio.

Nan and Flossie unpacked the basket and spread the food on the table. Maria's and Tony's eyes widened with astonishment and pleasure at the sight of the dainty chicken sandwiches, iced cup cakes, and fruit.

"This is dreamy!" Nan sighed.

The sun filtered through the branches of the palm trees and the sound of the water from the fountain splashing into the shallow pool filled her with contentment.

When the lunch was finished, Maria jumped up to clear away the remains while Mrs. Bobbsey settled back in her chair with a book.

"Come on," Bert said, standing up. "Let's start our search for the package."

Led by Tony, the children trooped through the house. They looked in all cupboards and closets for the mysterious package but found nothing resembling it.

"If the package was stolen, I don't think anyone would hide it in the house," Nan said finally. "Why don't we search the grounds?"

They went into the garden and looked carefully under all the bushes and around the base of the wall.

Tony watched them admiringly. "You are very good detectives!" he observed. The twins had almost completely circled the wall when they reached the stretch behind the house. Suddenly Nan stopped.

"Look at those black scratches," she said to Bert, indicating a portion of the wall.

Bert ran up to examine the marks on the whitewash. "It looks as if someone had climbed over the wall!" he exclaimed.

"But why would anyone do that? And where would he go?" Tony asked.

"I don't know, but maybe we can find out," Bert replied. "Come here, Freddie!" he called. "I'll boost you up to the top of the wall, and you tell us what you see."

Freddie hurried over. Bert and Tony each held one of his legs and lifted him until he could perch on the broad top of the wall.

"Any signs of a person jumping down on the outside?" Bert asked.

Freddie surveyed the ground. "Yes," he declared. "The grass is real flat here." Then he exclaimed, "That windmill is quite near! And there's a little path to it from this wall!"

"Let's follow it!" Bert cried. "I'm coming up!"

"I want to go too!" Flossie pleaded.

"And so do I," Nan declared.

"Okay!"

Bert and Tony boosted Flossie to the top beside her twin, then helped Nan climb up. Finally the two older boys scrambled up. They dropped to the ground on the other side. Nan jumped beside them, then helped the younger twins down.

The five children walked single file along the faint path. It led them to the side of the mill. Once more the children went into the old building. It was still empty.

As they started back to the house, Tony let

Nan and the younger twins go ahead. Then he said to Bert in a low voice, "You like to watch at mill tonight? Maybe person who left package will bring something else to hide there."

"That's a good idea, Tony! You're getting to be a real detective!"

The Portuguese boy looked proud at Bert's praise. The two boys decided to wait until dark, then go up to the mill and keep watch all night.

The children played in the garden until late that afternoon. By the time the sun set, the air had turned cool.

"Come into the kitchen," Tony suggested. "My mother is cooking and there will be a fire."

The children exclaimed with pleasure when they entered the big room. The floor was stone and along one side was a huge open fireplace with a low fire burning in it. Bright curtains printed with birds and flowers hung at the windows.

There was a small gas stove and an old-fashioned sink with a force hand pump at one side. A large carved wooden table stood in the center of the room. It was set with brilliantly decorated earthenware bowls.

"It's bee-yoo-ti-ful!" Flossie cried.

"Something smells good!" Freddie observed.

"It's our Portuguese sausage and rice that my mother cooks," Tony explained.

"The fire is nice," Nan remarked gratefully as she walked over to watch Maria's preparations.

Freddie spied a hand bellows on the hearth by the fireplace. "That fire doesn't look very high," he thought. "I'll stir it up."

He picked up the bellows in both hands and gave it a hard squeeze. The blast of air hit the ashes in the bottom of the fireplace. They rose in a cloud and covered Freddie's face and head with black and gray specks!

"Freddie! You're a sight!" Flossie cried.

Nan added, "Put the bellows down and wash your face and hands."

"Okay!" Freddie dashed to the sink, climbed on a stool and began to move the pump handle up and down roughly.

"Não, não, pare!" Maria cried when she saw him.

The next second the pump handle came off in Freddie's grasp! The water continued to flow into the sink.

Freddie looked frightened. "I—I'm sorry!" he stammered.

Tony ran up. "No harm," he said consolingly. "Water will stop. Pump needs fixing. That is why my mother shout!"

By this time the water had stopped pouring into the sink. Maria filled a basin with warm water from a kettle on the stove, and Freddie washed his face.

When Mrs. Bobbsey came into the kitchen and heard of Freddie's mishap she laughed. "A shampoo for you before you go to bed, young man!"

Maria assigned places at the table, and they all sat down. While Tony held the pot, Maria ladled large portions of the savory rice and sausage into the bowls. This, with fresh bread and glasses of cold milk, was the supper.

"It's delicious, Maria!" Mrs. Bobbsey told her.

After Tony translated, Maria beamed at the praise.

By the time the dishes had been washed, the children were yawning. Maria smiled and beckoned them to follow her. The bedrooms were on the second floor, opening off a balcony which overlooked the patio.

The housekeeper showed Bert and Freddie to a room in the rear of the house. The two rooms she had prepared for Mrs. Bobbsey and the girls were in the front, overlooking the road.

"Ooh, look, Nan!" Flossie's eyes sparkled as she saw the huge double bed. It had four richly carved posts supporting a canopy. Heavy embroidered curtains covered the end and both sides.

"Are we going to sleep in here?" asked Flossie.

She ran across the room, pulled the curtains aside, and peered in. "It looks like a big box."

Mrs. Bobbsey pulled the curtains back and fastened them to the four posts. "You'll have more air with these open," she said as she kissed her daughters good-night.

The girls undressed quickly and jumped into bed. They fell asleep almost at once. Some time later a noise awakened Flossie. She lay still a second and listened. Then she shook Nan.

"What is it?" Nan asked sleepily. "Did you have a nightmare?"

"No," Flossie whispered. "A motor bike just stopped in front of here!"

CHAPTER XII

MIDNIGHT WATCH

"ARE you sure you heard a motor bike?" Nan asked Flossie. "Who could it be?"

The two girls listened in the darkness, but no sound broke the stillness. "I'm going to get up and look out the window," Nan said finally.

Flossie scrambled from the bed and followed Nan to the window overlooking the road. There was a moon but at the moment it was partially behind a cloud. The children could see the gate. It was closed, and there was no sign of anyone on the road.

"You must have been dreaming, Flossie," Nan decided finally, turning back toward the bed.

"Maybe whoever it was came into the house!" Flossie whispered.

"No one could get in," Nan declared. "I saw Maria lock the front door when we came upstairs. But, if you like, I'll go out on the balcony and see if there's anyone in the patio."

"I'll come with you."

Quietly Nan opened the door. The two girls crept out onto the balcony which ran around the inner wall of the house. They hung over the railing and peered down into the patio below. The moon had come out again. They could see the fountain and the pots of flowers, but no sign of any person.

"I'm going down and look around," Nan declared.

"Ooh! Do you think you should?" Flossie's voice quivered.

"I'm sure no one sneaked in here, but you stay upstairs," Nan advised.

But Flossie did not want to do this. She followed Nan down the stairs from the balcony to the patio. The two girls walked around the edge, peering into the rooms as they passed.

"See, there's no one here," Nan said.

Flossie shivered. "Maybe he's hiding. Let's go back to bed!"

The girls scurried up the stairs, closed the door to their room, and climbed into the big bed. They lay there whispering. The moon shining in the window made the room very light.

Suddenly Flossie grabbed Nan's hand and pointed toward the door. It was slowly opening!

White fingers curved around the door jamb.

Flossie pulled the sheet over her head and lay quaking. Nan watched wide-eyed as the door opened farther. Mrs. Bobbsey appeared.

"Mother!" Nan cried, sitting up in bed and pulling the sheet from Flossie's head. "You scared us!"

"I'm sorry, dear," her mother said. "I thought I heard someone out on the balcony and was afraid something was wrong. Were you up?"

"I heard a motor bike stop out in front," Flossie spoke up. "Nan and I went on the balcony and looked all around but we didn't see anyone."

"Flossie thought maybe the person on the bike came into the house," Nan explained.

"I don't think anyone would come here at this time of night. Try to go back to sleep." Mrs. Bobbsey went out and closed the door.

In the meantime, Bert had waited until the house was quiet and Freddie asleep. Then he slid out of bed and put on his clothes.

"I wish I'd had time to buy another flashlight," he thought as he left the room. "It would come in handy tonight."

Bert tiptoed downstairs. Tony was waiting in the kitchen. "I have the key to the gate," he whispered, "so we won't have to climb over the wall. Come on!"

The two boys quietly left the house and walked to the front gate. Tony unlocked it, and they went out. They made their way around the outside of the wall, then up the hill to the windmill. Everything was quiet and the mill seemed deserted and ghostly in the moonlight.

"Where shall we hide?" Tony asked.

Bert spotted a clump of low bushes near the old building. "Here!" he motioned Tony to join him. The boys crawled under the bushes and sat down.

From their station they could look down on the quinta and the surrounding country. For a long time nothing happened. Then in the distance they saw a light moving along the winding road. As it grew nearer, the putt-putt of a motor bike reached their ears.

"It is strange," Tony remarked. "Who would be out in the country so late at night?"

The boys watched the motor bike draw up and stop in front of the quinta. The motor was turned off. At that moment the moon slid behind a cloud.

"Who can it be?" Bert asked in a low voice. "Do you think we should go down?"

"No, wait! Perhaps it is the thief and he will come here."

Bert and Tony sat quietly and watched the hillside in front of them. Some time passed. Then

"Who would be out in the country so late
at night?" Tony said

suddenly Bert put his hand on Tony's arm.

"Someone's coming!" he whispered.

The sound of light footsteps grew louder. Bert stood up cautiously. "We'll jump him when he gets opposite us," he said to Tony.

"Okay," the Portuguese boy whispered.

They waited breathlessly. Just as Bert was ready to spring, the moon came out from behind the cloud. It shone directly on the person coming up the path.

"Freddie!" Bert gasped. "What are you doing here? We thought you were the thief!"

"I woke up and you were gone," Freddie explained. "I heard Tony ask you before supper if you didn't want to watch the mill tonight. So I decided you were up here." He paused, then added reproachfully, "You knew I'd want to come with you, Bert!"

"Sorry, but you were fast asleep and I didn't want to wake you."

"Have you seen anybody up here?" asked Freddie.

"Not yet, but we did hear a motor bike stop in front of the house. We don't know whether anyone went in or not."

"I think I saw someone," Freddie declared. He explained that as he had come out the front door of the house, he thought he saw a man drop from the wall onto the road. "It was pretty dark, **though,**" he admitted.

"The man on the motor bike!" Bert exclaimed. "Let's go!" He began to run down the hill, the others close behind him.

When they reached the quinta they searched the road in front. The motor bike was gone!

"But how did it get away without our hearing it?" Bert asked in astonishment.

"Maybe something frighten man and he push bike away," Tony suggested.

"Well, he's gone anyway," Bert declared. "We might as well go back to bed."

The Bobbsey boys said good-night to Tony and crept up to their bedroom. They undressed in the dark and climbed into bed.

The next morning when Bert and Freddie came down to the kitchen for breakfast Tony was there. Mrs. Bobbsey and the girls were talking to him.

"Tony says you heard the motor bike last night too!" Nan called to her twin.

Excitedly the children compared their experiences of the night before. Bert and Freddie were surprised to hear that Nan and Flossie had been up looking for an intruder.

"It would have been funny if we'd all bumped into one another!" Flossie giggled. She felt much braver now that there was sunlight and the others were around.

"I'm the only one who saw the man!" Freddie boasted.

Bert rumpled his brother's hair. "You said you weren't sure!" he teased.

At that moment a piercing scream came from the living room. "My mother!" Tony cried and dashed from the kitchen.

The Bobbseys followed him. When they reached the living room they saw Maria standing by the case containing the collection of glass and china. She was wringing her hands and weeping.

"What is the matter, Maria?" Mrs. Bobbsey asked kindly.

The housekeeper pointed to the glass case and burst into another torrent of tears. The Bobbseys looked helplessly at Tony.

The boy spoke to his mother in Portuguese, then turned to the Americans. "The four gold ships have been stolen!" he cried.

"Then I *did* see a man last night!" Freddie burst out. "He stole the ships!"

"And there *was* someone here when we were looking around, Nan!" Flossie said.

"Yes, he must have run out after we went back upstairs," Nan agreed. "That was when Freddie saw him."

"Ask your mother if anything else is missing," Bert suggested to Tony.

Maria stopped crying long enough to look through the glass cases. She reported that the ships seemed to be the only articles that had been taken.

"Maybe the thief left a clue of some sort," Nan remarked. "Let's look."

Bert and Tony ran out to the garden. They discovered a man's footprints in the soft earth of the flower beds along the front wall. There were also marks on the wall where he had climbed over.

"Gate unlocked, but he climb over!" Tony chuckled.

"Perhaps it was Manuel Silva," said Bert. "When he stole the tile picture and the other ship, the gate was locked. So he didn't even try it this time! I wonder if he saw our car and guessed we were in the house. He's very daring."

The boys reported their findings to the others. Freddie and Flossie continued walking slowly around the patio, peering at the paving stones. Freddie picked up something at the edge of the pool.

"Look at this!" he called.

He held out a piece of candy!

CHAPTER XIII

THE WALLED TOWN

"CANDY!" Nan exclaimed. "Where did it come from? Could Mr. Machado have left it here?"

Tony shook his head. "Mr. Machado not eat candy. And my mother and I have no money to buy it," he added wistfully.

"It *must* have been Manuel Silva who broke in here last night," said Bert.

"Yes," Tony agreed. "My mother said he was eating candy when he came to see Mr. Machado!"

Mrs. Bobbsey spoke up. "I think this third theft should be reported to the police. You can tell them the clues you have found."

It was decided that she would drive the children into Magros to make their report. Maria and Tony would stay at the quinta to continue packing Mr. Machado's belongings.

Mrs. Bobbsey had another suggestion. "If we can stay here another night, we might do some sightseeing. I'd like to drive to Obidos. It is said to be a very interesting town."

Tony told his mother what Mrs. Bobbsey had said. The Portuguese woman nodded her head and beamed in delight.

When they arrived in Magros, Bert and Nan went into police headquarters. Officer Dias was interested to hear their account of the happenings at the Quinta do San Francisco.

"Some of the people in town have reported seeing lights there at night since Mr. Machado has left," he said. "Perhaps these lights have something to do with the recent thefts in this area. We will try to watch the quinta."

With Bert and Nan in the car again, Mrs. Bobbsey turned toward Obidos. She explained to the twins that it was a walled town of the sixteenth century.

As they drove along, the children were delighted to see smiling men with flat hats tending the flowers which bordered the road. When the car passed, the peasants stopped their work and gave a courteous salute.

"Aren't they nice men?" Flossie cried, leaning out of the car to wave.

"Yes, they are," Mrs. Bobbsey agreed. In a

little while she added, "That must be Obidos." She had just rounded a corner. A cluster of white houses surrounded by a high wall appeared on a hill before them.

"It looks like a ship!" Bert exclaimed. The walls came to a point at the highest spot and jutted out into the plain very much like the prow of a vessel.

"Everything in Portugal seems to have something to do with ships," Nan observed.

"Oh, look!" cried Flossie. "We have to go into the town through a gate."

Mrs. Bobbsey drove up to the square tower which formed the entrance to Obidos. The road passed through a very narrow arch, just wide enough for one car.

At that moment the entrance was blocked by a large American automobile trying to enter. The fat man behind the wheel was puffing as he inched the car forward and back, trying to drive it through the narrow opening. A crowd of Portuguese children called out advice as they hopped about excitedly.

The harder the man worked, the more difficult the task became. He finally leaned back in the seat and dropped his hands at his sides. He looked at Mrs. Bobbsey and shook his head hopelessly.

"Perhaps you can help him, Bert," Mrs. Bobbsey suggested. "He can't see how near he is to the walls and he can't understand those children."

Bert and Freddie hopped from the car and went over to the man. "May we direct you, sir?" Bert asked politely.

The American grinned and sat up. "You sure can, my boy!" he exclaimed. "This is the narrowest gate I've ever seen. It was never built for cars as big as mine."

Bert ran to the front of the car while Freddie took up his position by the rear bumper. The man grasped the wheel once more. Then, with Bert and Freddie calling out each time he reached the stone sides, he finally managed to drive through the entrance.

"Thank you, boys," the man called. "I'm going to the Pousada to lunch. Maybe I'll see you there and I'll buy you some ice cream!" The boys grinned.

Mrs. Bobbsey's small car went through the entrance easily and they came out onto the main street of the little town. It was lined with white houses, which were built so close together that they seemed almost to overlap. Yet each one had a balcony and a small terrace. All had window boxes filled with bright flowers.

"It's bee-yoo-ti-full" Flossie cried.

Her mother drove slowly down the narrow, winding street. Finally they reached the end.

The American's big car was parked at the curb.

"That must be the Pousada," Nan remarked, indicating an old building which looked like a fortified castle looming above them.

"It's what looked like the prow of a ship from a distance!" Bert exclaimed. "Let's go up."

Mrs. Bobbsey parked the car, and they began the climb to the castle. The cobbled lane zigzagged back and forth until it ended in a paved courtyard. A steep flight of stone steps led up to a doorway.

The heavy door swung open easily and the Bobbseys stepped into a panelled hall. To their right they could see a large room. The walls were covered with huge tapestries.

"It does look like a castle!" Bert exclaimed. "I wonder what *pousada* means."

A dignified-looking man, holding several menu cards, opened the door to their left. Behind him the children could see tables covered with snowy tablecloths.

The man had heard Bert's remark. "Ah, you are Americans!" he remarked in English. *"Pousada* is the Portuguese word for inn. The government has turned many of the old castles into *pousadas* so that everyone may enjoy them."

"It looks lovely," Mrs. Bobbsey said with a smile. "May we have lunch here?"

"Yes, indeed." The man led the family into the

dining room and to a table near a window. "I will give you a waiter who speaks English," he said.

As they walked toward the table, Bert noticed two men seated nearby. They were in deep conversation, but when they saw the Bobbseys coming, one man shook his head at the other. Both stopped talking abruptly.

A waiter hurried up to the Bobbseys' table. "Good afternoon," he said. "I am glad to practice my English. I will tell you what the menu says."

He began to translate. Bert's glance fell on the two men at the next table. They seemed to have relaxed and were now talking again in Portuguese.

Mrs. Bobbsey and the twins gave their luncheon order and the waiter left. The conversation at the next table grew louder. The men seemed to be arguing about something. It was impossible not to overhear some of the words.

Suddenly Nan looked excited. She turned and spoke to Bert. "That one man has repeated '*Magros*' and '*moinho*'—mill—several times."

Bert nodded. "I heard him. He has also said 'Saturday' and something which sounds like '*as ooma.*'"

"Do you suppose they could be talking about Mr. Machado's windmill?" Nan suggested.

"Maybe they're part of the gang which has been stealing things in this area. I'm sure the windmill must be involved."

After the Bobbseys finished their main course, the waiter brought in plates of ice cream for everyone. "The gentleman by the door sent this to you," he said, beaming.

The twins looked over. Their fat friend with the large automobile smiled and waved to them. While this was going on, the two men at the next table paid their bill and left the dining room.

When the children were ready to leave they stopped to thank the man for their dessert. "If it hadn't been for you," he teased, "I would never have been able to drive into this town! Thank you again."

"Oh, you're very welcome," said Bert, and Freddie grinned.

Nan went ahead. As she crossed the hall, she said, "Let's look in here," and entered the large room. The others followed her.

"Those men again!" Bert said in a low tone. The two Portuguese were strolling about, picking up various articles on display and examining them.

The twins walked around the room, admired the view over the countryside from the windows, then went back to the car.

"Will you stop at the Magros police headquarters again, Mother?" Bert asked as they left Obidos. He told Mrs. Bobbsey and the younger twins what he and Nan had overheard in the dining room.

"We think we may have found a clue!" Nan added.

Officer Dias was interested in the story which Bert and Nan told him. "Can you give me a description of these men?" he asked.

"One was tall and blond," Nan said. "The other was dark and medium height."

"Aha!" the policeman cried. "One of the men suspected of the thefts from the castles is tall and blond! Can you tell me anything else you overheard?"

"They kept repeating something which sounded like *as ooma*," Bert remarked. "What would that mean?"

"It could have been *as uma*," Dias said. "That would mean 'at one o'clock.' "

"That's it!" Bert cried. "They were planning to meet at the mill Saturday at one o'clock!"

"One o'clock in the morning or afternoon?" Nan wondered.

"I would suspect one in the morning," Dias said slowly. "They would hardly meet in daylight. I will have my men there at that time!"

Back in the car Bert and Nan told the others what the officer had said.

Freddie was excited. "Let's go to the mill and help him catch the bad men!" he proposed.

Mrs. Bobbsey shook her head. She reminded the children that their father would be back in Lisbon on Saturday and that they were due to fly to the United States on Sunday.

"Then we have only four more days to find the quinta tile picture!" Nan cried.

"And to solve the cock-a-doodle-doo mystery!" Flossie giggled.

A tasty supper prepared by Maria was waiting for them when they reached the quinta again. Tony was amazed to hear about the latest happenings in the mystery.

"If the *polícia* catch the men, you will be the reason," the Portuguese boy said admiringly.

"But we won't know!" Freddie wailed.

Tony promised that he would ask Officer Dias to telephone the Bobbseys in Lisbon and let them know the result of the watch at the mill.

Mrs. Bobbsey was eager to get back to Lisbon, so the next morning they all gathered in the kitchen for an early breakfast. When they had finished, Bert and Freddie brought down the bags.

Tony looked sad as he said good-by. "Now I cannot be detective any more," he remarked.

"Sure you can, Tony," Bert said cheerfully.

"You'll probably be able to find another mystery around here to solve!"

With Maria and Tony standing in the doorway waving to them the Bobbseys made their way to the front gate.

"Why, where's the car?" Mrs. Bobbsey asked in bewilderment. The black automobile with the green stripe was not parked by the wall!

"There it goes!" Bert yelled. He pointed to a car some distance down the road.

Bert raced after it, but the sedan picked up speed and disappeared around a curve!

CHAPTER XIV

THE WARNING

"SOMEBODY is stealing our car!" Flossie cried. The others were too surprised to speak. A second later Bert returned, puffing from his run.

"I couldn't catch him," he said. "I couldn't even get near enough to see what the driver looked like!"

"Now how are we going to get back to Lisbon?" Mrs. Bobbsey asked.

Tony spoke up eagerly. "I go into Magros and find another automobile for you!" He explained that there was an old bicycle at the quinta which the gardener had left there. He would ride that into Magros and send a car out for the Bobbseys.

"That would be very nice. Thank you, Tony." Mrs. Bobbsey gave a sigh of relief, but said she was worried about the rented car.

She and the older twins went into the patio to wait. Freddie and Flossie meanwhile started a game of tag in the garden. Almost an hour later Freddie dashed into the courtyard, his eyes blazing with excitement.

"Come see what Tony's brought!" he cried. He turned and ran back outside, his mother, sister, and brother following him. They stopped in surprise when they reached the gate.

Tony sat proudly holding the reins of a gaily harnessed horse. Flowers bobbed over its ears and bright colored ribbons were tied to the leather. The cart was a high, two-wheeled affair with a seat across the front and one running lengthwise along each side.

"Where's the car?" Bert finally asked when he had recovered from his surprise.

"No car in village," Tony explained. He went on to say that the cart and horse belonged to a neighbor. The man had agreed to lend them to the Bobbseys. They could be left with his brother, who lived in Lisbon.

"We-ll, I don't know," said Mrs. Bobbsey.

"Oh, please, Mommy," Flossie pleaded, *"please* let's go in the cart!"

"I'll drive, Mother," Bert volunteered. He had often driven horses on his Uncle Daniel's farm.

"All right," Mrs. Bobbsey agreed. She

climbed up on the driver's seat with Bert, while Nan got in back with Freddie beside her and Flossie just across. Tony put the bags in with them and once more waved good-by.

The horse was young and rather skittish, but Bert kept a firm hand on the reins and they made good time toward the city. Finally the pale colored houses of Lisbon came into view.

"We should be at the pensão by lunchtime," Mrs. Bobbsey observed. "We'll take a taxi when we leave the horse and cart."

At that moment came a roar behind them. Before Bert could pull the horse over to the side of the road a motor bike whizzed past.

The sudden noise startled their frisky horse. He began to run pellmell over the cobblestones! Bert hauled back on the reins and the horse's pace slackened. But suddenly there was a great jolt, as a wheel came off the cart and one side dropped to the road!

Flossie bounced into the air. She would have fallen over the back of the seat if Nan had not grabbed her just in time.

Mrs. Bobbsey had turned quickly. "Are you children all right?" she asked anxiously.

Nan assured her that no one had been hurt. They all climbed down from the cart. Bert ran across the road and brought back the big wheel from where it had rolled.

Nan grabbed Flossie just in time

"I don't know how to put this on," he admitted.

Nan frowned. "How are we going to get into Lisbon?"

"Let's hitch a ride!" Freddie spoke up.

"I'm afraid we'll have to." Mrs. Bobbsey peered up the road.

No private cars passed, but finally a truck approached. Bert stepped to the middle of the road and hailed it. The driver stopped. He shook his head when Bert spoke to him in English. But he got down and examined the cart and the wheel. In a moment he shrugged as if to say he could not fix it.

Desperate, Mrs. Bobbsey took a slip of paper from her purse. The owner of the cart had written his brother's name and address on it. She showed the slip to the man, pointed to her family and then toward the city.

A smile broke over the man's face. *"Sim, sim!"* he cried. He motioned the Bobbseys to climb into the truck.

Bert tied the horse to a nearby tree, then helped his mother and Nan up beside the driver. He boosted Freddie and Flossie into the back and scrambled up after them. The truck went on its way.

A short time later the driver stopped in front of a house. He pointed to the door and smiled.

"I guess we're here," Nan said.

"Obrigado! Thank you!" Mrs. Bobbsey and the twins called as they piled out and the driver started off.

A young woman answered Bert's knock. She looked at the group, then spoke in English. "You wish to see me?"

"I'm glad you speak English," said Mrs. Bobbsey, and explained about the damaged cart.

"I teach English in the school," the woman said. "I am sorry you have had such an experience. My husband is not at home, but I will tell him about the horse and cart when he returns."

Back at the pensão once more, Mrs. Bobbsey telephoned the car rental agency and reported the theft of the car. The man in charge promised to notify the police immediately.

"I'd like to work on the rooster mystery," said Nan. "How about our going down to the cabinet shop to see Carlos Pinto?"

When the twins arrived Carlos Pinto was working busily. "Come in!" he said cordially. "I haven't seen you for several days. How is your mystery coming along? Have you found your green rooster?"

"No, but we know what it is now," Nan told him.

Carlos was very interested when the children

told him about their adventures at Nazaré and the quinta.

"It does sound as if Manuel Silva is the thief," he said. "An antique tile picture such as you describe would be very valuable. Although tiles are still made in Portugal, the quality went down after the eighteenth century. The early ones of pale yellow and green are worth a great deal of money."

"We're going home next Sunday," Bert remarked. "I'd sure like to find that picture before then."

"If Manuel should come in here, I'll try to get word to you," Carlos promised.

The next morning Freddie and Flossie ran out into the garden before breakfast. They hung over the wall, watching the boats on the river.

"Bom dia!" A young boy ran up the steps from the street, a large tray balanced on his head. The tray was piled with small, tissue-wrapped objects. With a wave of his hand the boy hurried through the door into the kitchen.

"Those are the rolls we have for breakfast!" Flossie remarked. "Come on, it's time to eat!"

The younger twins found Mrs. Bobbsey, Nan, and Bert already at the table. "We saw the rolls come, so we knew it was breakfast time!" Freddie announced as he slid onto his chair.

Nan picked up the roll the waitress had just put on her plate. "They look good," she remarked as she began to remove the tissue.

She gazed at the paper more closely. "That's queer! There's writing on it!"

"Let's see it." Bert took the paper from his sister. *"Va embora,"* he read. "What does that mean?"

Judy was going through the dining room. Nan called to her and held out the tissue. "What do these words mean?" Nan asked.

"It's Portuguese for 'go away,'" Judy replied, "but I don't understand why anyone would write on that paper."

After Judy left Nan looked at Bert. "I think Manuel Silva wrote those words. He knows we're looking for the green rooster and he wants us to leave Portugal!"

"If he's in Lisbon, we'll find him!" Bert declared. "He's probably not in his room. I wonder where else he might be."

Flossie spoke up. "We could look in a candy store!"

Nan hugged her little sister. "That's a great idea, honey!" she said. "I think I saw a shop that sold candy right next to the house where Manuel lives. We'll go there!"

The twins were about to leave the pensão when Mrs. Bobbsey was called to the telephone. She was smiling as she returned.

"That was the police," she told the twins. "The car was found at the edge of town late last night. It was out of gas but not damaged. The police will bring it around this morning."

"I'll bet Manuel stole it!" Bert exclaimed. "He got back to Lisbon ahead of us. If he came to the quinta on a motor bike the other night, he could have put the bike in the back of the car before he drove back to town."

The children talked excitedly as they ran down the street. Nan pointed out the shop where candy was sold, and they hurried inside.

The store shelves were a mass of color. All kinds of figures made of pottery in brilliant shades of red, blue, and green stood on them.

"Ooh, doesn't the candy look yummy?" Flossie cried, running over to admire the glass case full of sweets.

The candies were made in the shapes of fish, shells, and birds. Some even looked like tiny loaves of bread.

A dark-haired young girl came up to the children. She spoke to them in English. "You like candy?" Flossie bobbed her head enthusiastically.

Nan bought a box of assorted pieces, then asked, "Do you know a man named Manuel Silva? I think he lives next door."

"Oh, yes," the clerk replied. "Manuel is a very good customer. He was here this morning and bought several boxes of candy. He said he was leaving Lisbon and wanted some to take with him."

The girl looked past the children toward the street. "There he is now!"

Bert dashed to the door. "Come on!" he called to the others. "Now is our chance to talk to him!"

Manuel was several doors away by the time the twins reached the street. He was strolling along looking in the shopwindows. The four children began to run after him.

The heavy-set man evidently heard the footsteps behind him. He turned and saw the children. At once he walked faster, crossed the street, and darted into a church.

"Now we've got him!" Bert cried. "He can't get away from us in there!"

The children hurried across the street and up the steps of the church. They looked around the whitewashed interior.

Manuel Silva was not there!

CHAPTER XV

PURSUIT IN THE DARK

"BUT he must be in here!" Nan cried.

The church was small. The altar of blue and white tiles stood out against whitewashed walls. The candles wore little wreaths of colored wax flowers. Except for their flickering light, the church was dark.

At that moment a young priest came up to the children. "Are you looking for someone?" he asked in English.

Bert explained that a man they suspected of being a thief had run into the church. "Is there any way he could have left except by the doors in front?" the boy asked.

The priest shook his head. "There is a rear door, but it is kept locked. Come, I will walk around with you while you look for this man."

The four children and the priest made their way slowly through the church, peering into all the nooks and looking under the pews. Manuel Silva was not in sight.

138

In the rear wall behind the altar Bert spied the outlines of a door. "Where does that lead?" he asked.

The priest explained that the door opened onto steps down to the old foundations of the building. "This church is only about one hundred years old," he said. "It is built on part of the remains of a sixteenth century church."

"Things around here are pretty old, aren't they?" Freddie remarked, thinking of the ancient building in which the pensão was lodged.

"Not many of our original buildings are left," the priest said sadly. "Lisbon had a great earthquake in 1755, and most of the city was destroyed."

"How awful!" Nan shuddered. Then she had a thought. "Could Manuel have hidden down there in the foundations?"

"It is possible. One moment." The priest went into a room at one side and returned with a flashlight. "We shall see. That space is never used."

He opened the door and shone the light onto the crumbling stone steps. The children followed him down into the cold, damp underground room. No one was there.

"It appears that your thief has escaped," the priest remarked as they climbed the steps again.

Discouraged, the twins thanked the kind

priest and left the church. Back at the pensão, they found Judy working in the garden. She greeted them with a smile.

"You have been very busy children since you came to stay with us," she remarked. "Have you been exploring Lisbon?"

"We're trying to solve a cock-a-doodle-doo mystery!" Flossie said with a giggle.

Seeing Judy's bewildered expression, Nan told her about the tile picture which had been stolen from the quinta and their efforts to find it.

"Perhaps the thief has already sold the picture," Judy suggested.

"If he has, we may never find our green rooster!" Nan cried.

Judy looked thoughtful. "I've seen antique tiles in the gift shop connected with the Folklore Restaurant. Maybe the man who runs it could tell you where to look for yours. He speaks English."

Judy told the twins they would find the restaurant interesting. It was famous for the native dancing and singing which it provided for the guests' entertainment.

"Oh, I want to see it!" said Flossie.

When Mrs. Bobbsey heard about Judy's suggestion, she agreed to take the children to the restaurant for dinner that evening.

They found the gift shop to the left of the restaurant entrance. "Two of you come with me to the dining room and we'll get a table while the other two go into the shop," Mrs. Bobbsey suggested.

"Nan," said Bert, "why don't you and Freddie go with Mother? Flossie and I will see what we can find out."

The gift shop owner was a very pleasant man. He listened to Bert's story with great interest. "I was offered a picture like that just this morning," he said.

"You were! Did you buy it?" Bert asked. He was excited to think that their search might be at an end.

"No. The man who had it wanted too much money."

"Was he short and fat?" Flossie spoke up.

The shop owner shook his head. "No. But he said he was selling the picture for a friend. He left an address where he can be reached in case I changed my mind."

"Will you give it to us?" Bert asked eagerly.

The man took a card from a table drawer. "Here it is. The address is in the old section of Lisbon called the Alfama. I hope the picture turns out to be the one you're looking for."

Bert and Flossie thanked the shopkeeper for his help and went into the restaurant. Mrs.

Bobbsey, Nan, and Freddie were at a table near the stage, which stretched across one end of the room. The place was almost filled with diners. Waiters in peasant costume bustled about with trays of delicious-looking food.

The others were eager to hear what Bert and Flossie had found out. "I'll drive you to the Alfama tomorrow morning," Mrs. Bobbsey promised after hearing what the gift-shop owner had said.

As they waited for dinner, the twins settled back and gazed around the dining room.

"Look at that boy!" Flossie said to her twin.

Standing a few tables away was a boy about Freddie's height. He was dressed in tight black knee pants, a short red jacket, and a ruffled white shirt. On his head was a little black velvet stocking cap complete with tassel.

While Freddie and Flossie watched him, the boy took an ashtray from a table and replaced it with a clean one. Then he moved on to the next table. He looked very serious.

"Hi!" said Freddie when the Portuguese boy arrived at the Bobbseys' table.

"*Olá,*" the Portuguese boy replied, but he did not smile.

The Bobbseys had almost finished their dinner by the time the boy came to their table again.

"*Olá,*" said Flossie with a friendly look.

This time the little waiter smiled shyly. At that moment the lights in the dining room were dimmed. A man came out on the stage and announced that the folk dances would begin.

A group of young men and girls in gay peasant costumes ran onto the stage. The musicians began a tune, and the dance started.

"I love this!" Nan said enthusiastically. She and the others were so interested in what was taking place on the stage that they did not see Freddie slip away.

Flossie turned to speak to her twin. "Where did he go?" she asked in surprise.

"I see him!" Bert chuckled. At the far side of the room Freddie, in the other boy's red jacket, was busy playing his part and emptying ashtrays! The Portuguese lad leaned against the wall, watching.

"Goodness!" said Mrs. Bobbsey. "What will Freddie think of next? You'd better bring him back, Bert, before he gets into trouble!"

Freddie looked disappointed when Bert came over to him. "Luis traded jackets with me. He said I could do this!" Freddie protested.

"It's his job," Bert said. "Mother wants you to come back to our table."

Sadly Freddie changed jackets with the Portuguese boy again and followed his brother to the table. A dance was just ending.

Freddie was busy emptying ashtrays!

As the group was catching its breath, the master of ceremonies came to the microphone. "Our performers invite members of the audience to join in the final dance," he said in English. "Won't some of you come to the stage?"

Several couples got up. "Come on!" Nan jumped from her chair. "It sounds like fun!" Bert and the younger twins lost no time in following her.

When the children reached the stage, the dancers were holding up great hoops entwined with flowers. The leader of the dancers smiled at the twins. He gave each of them a flower hoop.

"I put the little couple behind me, then the older ones," he directed.

The dancers and the guests lined up in pairs. The orchestra began to play fast music and the parade started.

The first couple led the way down the steps from the stage, along the edge of the dining room, then across to the other side and up to the stage again. As they marched they sang.

The Bobbseys soon caught on to the rhythm. The people at the tables stood up and applauded as the line of flower hoops continued around the room.

Bert and Nan were singing lustily as they neared the door which led out into the lobby. Suddenly Bert stopped singing.

"Nan! That man in the doorway!" he exclaimed.

He was Pedro from Nazaré!

"What can we do?" Nan asked.

"When we get just past the door, step out of line. One of us can keep Pedro talking while the other calls the police."

Freddie and Flossie were having such a good time prancing along and singing that they did not notice Bert and Nan leave the line.

But as the older twins started toward Pedro, the man gave them a startled glance. He turned quickly and ran out through the lobby.

"Come on, Nan!" Bert cried. "He mustn't get away!"

Pedro dashed out the front door, with Bert and Nan close behind him. It was dark outside, but Pedro did not hesitate. He turned to the right and disappeared around the corner.

Bert and Nan followed. They found themselves in a narrow, cobblestoned street. They could hear Pedro's feet pounding up ahead in the darkness. They raced after him.

A minute later Bert stopped. "We're never going to catch him this way," he panted.

"What can we do?"

"It wasn't dark when we drove to the restaurant," Bert reminded her. "I remember noticing how crooked these streets are. It seems to me that if we go up that lane over there, we can get to the next corner before Pedro does."

"Let's try it!" Nan started up the dark, narrow alleyway.

The twins could still hear Pedro in the distance. The sound grew fainter and then died away.

"Do you think we've missed him?" Nan asked anxiously.

"I'm sure he's up ahead!" Bert dashed on at full speed. He was just passing a narrow side street when something rolled out into his path.

Bert hit it and pitched headlong!

CHAPTER XVI

THE SECRET TUNNEL

"BERT!" Nan screamed when she saw her brother fall. "Are you hurt? What happened?"

Bert sat up groggily. "Something rolled out right in front of me," he gasped. "I couldn't stop!"

Nan walked over to a dark shape which had come to rest against a wall. She bent over to examine the object.

"It's a barrel!" she exclaimed. "Someone must have rolled it down that street on purpose to trip you!"

"Pedro!" Bert said as he slowly got to his feet. "Well, I guess we've lost him again. We may as well go back to the restaurant."

When Bert and Nan walked into the lobby of the Folklore, they found Mrs. Bobbsey and the young twins anxiously waiting for them.

"Goodness, Bert!" his mother exclaimed. "What happened to you?"

Looking down, Bert noticed for the first time that his slacks were torn at the knees and his hands skinned from the cobblestones.

"Where did you go?" Freddie asked. "I looked back to tell you something, and you and Nan were gone."

"We saw Pedro," Nan declared.

"Where?"

Bert and Nan described their chase and Bert's accident.

"I wonder what Pedro is doing in Lisbon?" Mrs. Bobbsey remarked. "You should notify the police, Bert."

"He may have come to meet Manuel," Bert suggested. "Wouldn't it be neat if we could catch them both? I'll call Officer Dias and tell him what we know."

When the Magros police chief heard the latest developments he said he would alert the Lisbon police to be on the lookout for both Manuel and Pedro. "You Bobbseys have been a great help to us," he said just before hanging up.

The next morning the Bobbseys set out for the Alfama. When they reached the old section of Lisbon, Mrs. Bobbsey parked the car.

Looking at the narrow, cobbled streets running uphill from the waterfront, she said, "I can't drive a car up there. I'll wait for you here."

Bert noticed the name of the street they were looking for painted on the side of an old building. The street consisted of broad steps and was just wide enough for the four children to walk abreast.

Waving good-by to their mother, the twins started up. They passed small shops with baskets of oranges and fish set out in front. Just inside the door of one shop an elderly woman sat knitting.

Bert held out the card with the address on it. *"Onde?"* he asked. Judy had told him that this meant "where."

The woman took the card. She puzzled over it for a minute, then called to someone. A young boy came from the back of the shop. He looked at the card, and with a friendly grin pointed farther along the street. He held up one finger, then put another across it in the form of a T.

"I think he means our house is on a corner," Nan told the others.

They smiled their thanks and continued the climb. There were no sidewalks. The house fronts were even with the roadway. Some had tiny iron balconies at the windows.

"Look at the pretty kitty," Flossie said. She ran up to pat a sleek-looking yellow cat stretched out on a window sill.

"Here's the number we're looking for," Bert called from the next corner.

The house was almost at the end of the street. Looking back, the children could see the broad Tagus River far below them.

Once inside the house, they found a narrow stairway which ran up from the tiny hallway. The "apartment 5" written on the card proved to be on the top floor.

Bert's knock was answered by a thin man with a black mustache. The Bobbseys were disappointed to see that he was not Manuel.

"Do you speak English?" Bert asked.

The man nodded.

"We understand that you have an antique tile picture," the boy said. "We are looking for one which was made of the Quinta do San Francisco."

"Ah, yes!" The man beamed. "I have just what you want! One moment!" He disappeared into the apartment.

"At last!" Nan sighed happily. "We've found the green rooster picture!"

The children waited impatiently for the man to return. In a few minutes he was back with a large picture made of tiles.

"See!" he said. "The Quinta do San Francisco made in sixteenth century!" He held it up for the children to see.

It was a picture of an estate. The tiles were a beautiful soft yellow and green, but there was no

"See!" he said. "The Quinta do San Francisco!"

border of animal tiles and no green rooster!

"I'm afraid it isn't the one we're looking for," Nan said finally.

Bert and Freddie were very disappointed, and Flossie was ready to cry. They managed to thank the man and made their way back down the stairs.

"I really thought we'd found it!" Bert said as they walked along the street toward the car.

"And we're leaving day after tomorrow," Nan said dolefully.

"I don't want to go home without the green rooster!" Flossie protested.

Mrs. Bobbsey could tell by the children's faces that the trip had not been successful. She tried to cheer them up on the drive back to the pensão, but they were too disappointed to talk much.

Finally, as they reached the Rua das Janelos Verdes, Bert spoke up. "Will you let me out at the church, Mother? I'd like to look around in there again."

"I'll go with you!" Freddie offered.

The boys found the young priest in the small room at the back of the church. He smiled a greeting.

"May my brother and I go down into that underground room again?" Bert asked. "We'd like to examine it."

The priest gave Bert his flashlight. "Be very careful," he cautioned.

Beaming the light before them, Bert and Freddie made their way down the stone steps. The dark cellar stretched before them.

"Wh-what are you looking for, Bert?" Freddie asked, his voice a little shaky.

"I'm sure there must be a way out of here," Bert replied. "Manuel couldn't have just disappeared, and I don't think he could have gone out the front door without our seeing him."

With Freddie close at his heels, Bert walked slowly beside the rough stone wall, shining the flash as he went. Several times he thought he saw an opening, but each time it proved to be only a break in the stone.

"Maybe we'd better go up, Bert," Freddie suggested. "It's awful spooky down here!"

"I'll go just a little farther," Bert said. "We must be almost at the end of the foundation."

Suddenly he stopped. "What's this?" He flashed the light at the wall just ahead. There was a smooth slab of stone with a wood lintel above it.

"It looks like a door!" Freddie cried.

"Hold the flash while I push!" Bert ordered. He thrust the light into Freddie's hand, then threw his weight against the stone. It moved easily! Bert stumbled into a dark passage beyond.

"A secret tunnel!" Freddie exclaimed in excitement.

"Let's see where it goes." Bert began to walk forward, shining the light ahead. Freddie followed.

The tunnel was narrow and just high enough for Bert to stand erect. The floor was rocky and uneven.

"It's cold down here!" Freddie declared.

Suddenly Bert stopped. "There's a big rock across the path," he called back to his brother. "I don't think we can go any farther."

The flashlight battery was growing weak and it was becoming difficult to see. The two boys turned around and hurried back the way they had come.

They closed the stone door behind them and made their way toward the stairs. Just as they reached them, the flash went out!

Bert and Freddie crept carefully up the steps. "Whew! I'm glad to get out of there!" Bert admitted as they gained the door into the church.

The priest was astonished when Bert told him about the secret door and tunnel. "There were many tunnels connecting buildings in the old days," he said. "You must have found one of them."

Bert was thoughtful as the boys walked to the pensão. "You remember Carlos Pinto told us there was supposed to be a tunnel leading out from his workshop?"

"Sure I do," said Freddie.

"I wonder if that tunnel under the church could be part of the same one?"

"Let's look again for the one in Carlos's shop!" Freddie proposed.

Nan and Flossie were excited to hear of the boys' discovery. "But I guess Manuel couldn't have escaped that way if the tunnel is blocked," Nan pointed out.

Bert mentioned his thought that the tunnel under the church might be the same one which was rumored to be under the pensão.

"But we looked in Carlos' shop and couldn't find any opening," Nan reminded him.

Seeing how discouraged the children were, Mrs. Bobbsey suggested a drive around the city for the afternoon.

"I guess I'll take Linda," Flossie announced. "She hasn't been out much since we came to Portugal." Flossie's doll Linda had gone with her on many trips, but there had not been much time for the little girl to play with her since landing in Lisbon.

After supper that evening Flossie suddenly

cried, "Linda! I left her in the car! She can't stay out there all night!"

"I'll get her, Floss," Bert offered. "The car's parked in front of the gate. It won't take a minute."

Bert ran down the stone steps, his rubber-soled shoes making no sound. As he reached the gate at the bottom he became aware of two men standing on the sidewalk outside. One was of medium height and quite slim while the other was short and very fat. They were speaking in English.

As Bert paused in the shadow of the wall, the fat man spoke. "I assure you I have the green rooster tile picture!"

CHAPTER XVII

GAMES AND GLUE

MANUEL! Bert pressed back against the wall. "Now I can find out where the picture is!" he thought.

The slim man spoke in a British accent. "My dear chap," he said, "I must have that picture soon. My customer in England won't wait forever!"

Manuel sounded worried. "I tell you I have the picture well hidden. It's not far away, and just as soon as the Americans leave, I'll get it for you!"

"What have the Americans to do with it?" the Englishman asked scornfully.

Manuel explained that he had seen the children in Pedro's shop in Nazaré and had heard them ask about the green rooster. "They have a crazy idea that it belongs to them and they might make trouble," the fat man said nervously.

He went on, "But I have a friend who is a waitress here at the pensão. She tells me the Americans are leaving Lisbon soon. You shall have the green rooster as soon as they are gone!"

"I think you're a bit balmy to be afraid of four children," the slim man sniffed, "but I'll wait until Sunday."

Still talking, the two men walked off down the street. Bert darted out to the car, grabbed Flossie's doll, and raced back up the stairs.

He found Mrs. Bobbsey and the other twins in the lounge. "Why were you gone so long?" his mother asked.

Bert gave Linda to Flossie, then told her and the others what he had overheard. "So now we *know* Manuel stole the green rooster and that it's hidden nearby!"

"But can we find it tomorrow?" Nan asked in despair. "It's our last chance!"

The next morning the Bobbseys gathered in the garden and tried to think of some way to locate the hiding place of the green rooster.

"Maybe Manuel has it in his room," Flossie suggested. "We could look there."

"We couldn't just break into his room, Flossie," her twin protested.

At that moment Judy came out to say that Officer Dias was calling from Magros and wanted to speak to Bert. The other children went inside with him and listened as he talked to the policeman.

"You caught the thieves at the mill last night?" Bert repeated. Flossie gave a little squeal of excitement.

Bert continued to listen for a while. The others could not hear what Officer Dias was saying, but Bert's answering remarks filled them with suspense.

Finally, with a "That's all right. We're glad we could help," he ended the conversation.

"Tell us what happened!" Nan urged as her twin turned from the telephone.

"Come into the lounge where Mother is and I'll give you the whole story," the boy replied.

Settled in comfortable chairs, the others listened as Bert began. "Our guess that the thieves were going to meet at the windmill at one o'clock this morning was right. Officer Dias and a couple of his men hid out there and caught four men as they were bringing some of their loot to hide."

Bert went on to report that the men were the ringleaders of a gang which had been stealing from the wealthy estate owners in the Magros district. Among the loot which the police had found in the mill were the four gold sailing ships stolen from the quinta.

"Marvelous!" said Nan. "Now Maria will feel better."

"Oh, another thing," Bert went on. "One of the men they caught was our friend Pedro!"

"So he *was* one of the gang!" Nan remarked. "He must have gone back to Magros yesterday."

"Officer Dias said that our report about the two men at Obidos had really broken the case for the police. He wanted me to tell you that they are very grateful."

"Their case turned out all right," said Freddie, "but what about ours?"

"Yes, we haven't found the cock-a-doodle-doo," Flossie said sadly.

"Why don't we go to Manuel's house again?" Nan proposed. "We might be able to get some clue to where he hid the picture."

"We can try," Bert agreed gloomily.

The twins started down the steps to the street. As they passed the cabinet shop, they looked in. Carlos was working at a table by the door. He was mumbling to himself and appeared to be disturbed.

"Is something wrong?" Bert called to the cabinet maker as they went by.

Carlos looked up. "Good morning," he said. "Yes. I am in trouble. One of my best customers has to have two inlaid tables by this evening and I don't see how I can finish them."

"Perhaps I could help," Bert suggested. "I've had Shop in school and know something about wood-working."

Carlos smiled. "I would appreciate it," he said. "I can show you how to do the inlay."

Bert turned to the other children. "We can go to Manuel's later."

"I'll help you too, Carlos!" Freddie offered.

The children went into the shop. Nan and Flossie watched with interest as Carlos demonstrated the art of inlay to the boys.

The man pointed to two table tops which lay on the workbench. About two inches from the edge on all four sides a groove had been cut in the dark wood.

"That is where we put the inlay," Carlos explained. He picked up a pot of glue and carefully brushed some into the groove. Then he selected a thin wooden strip of a lighter shade. With a small rubber-tipped hammer he tapped the strip into the hole.

"If you could do that on one of the tables it would be a great help," Carlos said, looking at Bert.

When the boy nodded, Carlos went on, "There are the top, four legs, and a drawer to be done for this table. The grooves have been made and the inlay cut. The second table is much more elaborate. I will do that one."

Freddie still insisted he wanted to help, so Carlos installed the boys at one workbench with table pieces, glue, and strips of inlay wood. Then

he went to work on the second table. Nan and
Flossie wandered out into the little courtyard to
wait.

Bert worked steadily, but Freddie was having
a hard time. First he got too much glue in the
groove and it oozed over the table leg on which
he was working. Then he picked up a piece of
the inlay and pounded it into the groove. When
it was finished, he found the piece was too
short!

"What'll I do, Bert?" he whispered, showing
his brother the result.

Quickly Bert seized a tool and pried out the
inlay before it had time to set. Then he found the
correct length piece and gave it to Freddie.

The little boy set his jaw and began again. He
carefully placed the strip in the groove and
began to pound. "I'll put it in real tight," he told
himself, "so it won't come out!"

Freddie raised the little hammer and brought
it down hard—on his finger! "Ow!" he yelled.

Bert and Carlos both jumped at the sound.
Freddie hopped up and down holding his finger.

"Here, stick it under the cold water!" Bert
ran to a faucet and turned it on.

"I'm sorry," Freddie said when the pain had
gone. "I guess I'm not a very good furniture-
maker!"

"You're all right," Bert assured him, "but I'll

"Ow!" yelled Freddie

tell you what would be a good idea. Why don't you take Nan and Flossie up to Manuel's house while I finish this job? You might be the one to find the tile picture."

"Okay." Freddie washed his hands and went out to the girls. A minute later Bert heard them running down the steps to the street.

Nan and the small twins found the landlady at Manuel's house leaning against the street door. She was talking to a neighbor. As the children came up, the other woman walked away.

"Is Manuel at home?" Nan asked.

The woman caught the word Manuel. *"Não, não,"* she replied, shaking her head. She held up two fingers and shook her head again.

"I think she means he hasn't been here for two days," Nan guessed.

The woman seemed to sense what Nan had said. She nodded vigorously. *"Sim,"* she said.

She pointed to the door, then up the street and shook her head. *"Polícia!"*

Nan looked puzzled. "Maybe she means the police couldn't find Manuel either!" Freddie suggested.

There seemed to be nothing more the children could do, so they made their way back to the cabinet shop. Carlos and Bert were still working at the benches. They were both interested to hear that Manuel could not be found.

"If you want to wait until I finish this table," Bert said, "I'll take you down to the church and show you the tunnel. I still think that may have something to do with the mystery."

"Okay," Flossie piped up. "Right now let's play hide-and-seek. This is a good place."

"You and Nan hide," Freddie directed. "See how fast I can find you."

The little boy leaned forward against one of the pillars, his head in his arms. "One, two, three—" he began to count.

Nan and Flossie tiptoed toward the back of the long room. Flossie saw a big slab of wood propped against one wall. Quickly she crawled behind it and crouched down.

Nan saw a space in the wall which looked as if it might have been a fireplace at one time. She crept to the far corner and stood there, her back pressed against the wall.

"Eight, nine, ten," Freddie counted. "Here I come, ready or not!"

The little boy walked quietly down the room peering behind all the pillars. Suddenly there was a giggle and Flossie jumped from behind the piece of wood. Before Freddie could turn, she raced to the pillar and touched it. "Home free!" she called.

The next minute Nan stepped from her hiding place and made for the pillar. But Freddie was too quick for her and tagged his sister's arm.

Flossie clapped her hands. "Now Nan's *It!* Freddie and I will hide."

Nan hid her face and started to count. Freddie, with an impish grin, crawled under the table where Bert was working. Flossie disappeared into the dim distance of the basement.

"Here I come!" Nan called as she completed the count and began her search.

"Home free!" Freddie shouted as he scurried from under the bench and touched the pillar.

The next second Flossie screamed!

CHAPTER XVIII

THE GREEN ROOSTER

AT the sound of the scream Nan dashed toward the rear of the long room. Bert, Freddie and Carlos ran after her.

"Where are you, Flossie?" Nan called.

"Here!" came a faint cry.

When Nan, Carlos and the boys reached the end of the basement, they saw a strange sight. A large stone in the rear wall had fallen, revealing a dark passageway behind it. Flossie was lying in the opening!

"Flossie! Are you hurt?" Bert ran forward and picked up his sister.

The little girl struggled to her feet. "I came way back here so Nan wouldn't find me," she explained. "I leaned against the wall and it fell in! I was s'prised, but I'm not hurt."

Carlos had been examining the opening.

"There's a tunnel here!" he exclaimed. "The old story of the secret passageway is true!"

The Bobbsey children crowded around and peered into the darkness. "This must be the other end of the tunnel leading from the church!" Bert cried. "I'll bet Manuel escaped this way the other day. He could have gone through your shop, Carlos, when you were busy and you wouldn't have noticed him!"

The cabinet-maker agreed that this was quite possible.

"Bert!" Nan cried. "You said Manuel told that man the green rooster picture was hidden near here! Perhaps it's in the tunnel!"

"Let's look!" Freddie started through the opening.

"Wait, young man!" Carlos cautioned. "I'll get some candles. My electricity often fails so I keep a supply."

In a few minutes he was back with a lighted candle for each twin. They followed him into the tunnel.

Like the passageway leading from the church, this one was narrow with a low ceiling. It was also cold and damp.

Carlos and the twins had gone about fifty feet when the tunnel widened into a small room. Bert raised his candle and peered around. Ranged along the walls were various pieces of furniture.

"So!" Carlos exclaimed. "Just as I suspected! Manuel was buying furniture from me and selling the pieces as antiques!"

"How can you tell?" Nan asked.

"He has stored the furniture in here where it is cold and damp. In a short time, the pieces will begin to look old."

"Manuel must have known about the entrance from your shop," said Bert.

"But where is the green rooster?" Flossie piped up.

They looked around. Nothing resembling a tile picture seemed to be in the room.

"What's this?" Nan walked over to a tall square package in one corner. It was heavy when she tried to pick it up.

"We will take this back to the shop and see." Carlos and Bert lifted the package and carried it to the tunnel entrance. They lugged the object into the shop and laid it on a workbench.

Bert picked up a knife from a tool chest and cut the cord which fastened the package. The heavy paper fell aside.

"It's tiles!" Freddie exclaimed.

"But not a picture," Flossie reminded him.

"Let's see what they are," Nan proposed, beginning to lay the separate tiles out on the table.

Freddie climbed to a stool and bent over the

workbench. He moved the tiles around. "Some of them are pictures of animals," he remarked. Then he picked up a soft yellow tile with a green figure on it.

"Here's a green rooster!" he shouted.

The others leaned forward eagerly. Nan looked closely at the tile Freddie held in his hand. "And there's an artist's name on it!" she cried.

"It's like a puzzle!" Flossie's blue eyes danced with excitement. "Let's put the pieces together!"

The tiles were spread out on the table and the twins went to work. Gradually a picture of the Quinta do San Francisco took shape. The animal tiles formed a border and the green rooster tile fitted into the lower right hand corner!

"We've found it! Hooray!" Flossie jumped down from her stool and began to dance around the room.

"I think I should report this to the police," Bert declared.

Carlos agreed and put in the call for the boy. In a short time an English-speaking officer arrived at the cabinet shop. Bert told him the whole story of the stolen green rooster picture.

The officer, who had introduced himself as Alberto Teixeira, grinned at the twins. "I would like to catch this Manuel Silva, as you say in

"Let's put the pieces together!" Flossie cried

America, 'with the goods.' If we could only trap him in the tunnel!"

"Couldn't you get Manuel to come here, Carlos?" Nan suggested.

"Perhaps." The two men and the children discussed the problem. It was finally decided that Carlos should send a note to Manuel at the restaurant where he usually ate. He would ask him to come to the shop to see a new piece of furniture. Then when Manuel came, Carlos would casually mention that the Americans had left the hotel.

"And we hope he comes back tonight to get the picture," Officer Teixeira said. "Then we arrest him 'with the goods!' "

"May we take the green rooster picture with us?" Bert asked. "We'd like to show it to our parents."

The officer agreed, saying that if the picture was needed in Lisbon for evidence, he would see that it was sent later to the Bobbseys in America.

Carlos quickly constructed a wooden rack to hold the loose tiles until they could be cemented together again. The children hurried up the steps to the pensão with Bert carefully carrying the precious picture.

"Daddy!" Flossie cried, seeing Mr. Bobbsey sitting with her mother under a tree. She ran across the garden to hug her father.

"I got here a few minutes ago," Mr. Bobbsey said, "and I've already heard about some of your exciting adventures."

"We found the green rooster!" Freddie blurted out.

"You did? Tell us about it!" Mr. Bobbsey motioned the children to sit down.

They threw themselves on the ground and began their exciting tale. They had just finished when the luncheon bell rang.

"I'm very proud of you all," Mr. Bobbsey declared as they walked toward the dining room. "You've solved two mysteries in the short time you've been here in Portugal!"

Just before supper Bert went down to see Carlos. The cabinet-maker said that Manuel had come to the shop and had appeared to be relieved when told that the American children had left.

"Teixeira suggests that you and Nan might like to hide with him tonight when he waits for Manuel," Carlos said.

"We sure would!" Bert beamed. "We'll be down as soon as it gets dark."

Carlos and the police officer were waiting in the shop when the twins arrived that night. Following the police officer's instructions, they took their places in a far corner of the room. The two men stationed themselves near the stone which concealed the tunnel opening.

"I hope Manuel comes soon," Nan whispered to her twin. "It's awfully dark and spooky in here!"

Nan had her wish. It was not long before they heard the sound of a key in a lock and the door of the shop swung open. A short, fat figure stepped into the room and beamed a flashlight around. Fortunately the light did not reach the shadowy depths where the two men and the twins were hiding.

The figure walked toward the rear of the shop, shining the light on the floor at his feet. There was a grating sound as he pushed the stone aside and stepped into the tunnel.

The next moment Teixeira and Carlos focused the man in the beam from their flashes. Manuel! Before the man could move, the officer had snapped handcuffs on his wrists.

He nudged Manuel sharply with his flash. "Get moving!" he ordered. "We're going up to the pensão where you will answer a few questions!"

Protesting, the fat man marched up the steps and into the lounge where Mr. and Mrs. Bobbsey, Freddie and Flossie were waiting.

"You may as well talk, Silva," the policeman advised. "Pedro and the rest of the gang have told us all about you. I think these children have some questions."

"How did you get into the quinta to steal the tile picture?" Bert asked him.

"I am not a thief. I am an antique dealer," Manuel said proudly. "I go around to estates to see the antiques. Mr. Machado would not sell the green rooster so I took a front door key I saw on his desk. Then I go back later when he has left for Brazil, climb the wall, unlock the door and take the picture! My English client had heard about it and wanted to buy it."

"You also stole the gold sailing ship!" Freddie spoke up.

"*Sim*. That I took to Pedro as a sample of the fine things to be had at the Quinta do San Francisco."

"Was it you who came to the quinta on the motor bike last Monday and took the other four gold ships?" Nan asked.

"And you stole our car, too!" Flossie accused him.

The fat man shrugged in acknowledgment. He said he had not realized anyone was staying at the quinta until he had seen Nan and Flossie come out onto the balcony. He had hidden the ships in the mill after the boys had gone back to the quinta later that night.

"But if you were going to sell the green rooster to the Englishman," Bert questioned, "why did you mention it in that note you dropped in Carlos's shop?"

"Is that why you came to Pedro's shop in Nazaré?" Manuel asked in amazement. "I wondered how you got on my trail."

"What about the note?" Bert insisted.

"I wanted to tell Pedro about the picture. If he had offered me enough money, I would have sold it to him rather than to the Englishman."

In reply to further questioning by Carlos and the Bobbseys, Manuel confessed that he had managed to have a duplicate key to the cabinet shop made. He had carried furniture into the tunnel at night to let it "age" as Carlos had suspected.

"When I found out you young ones were looking for the green rooster tile, I tried to keep you out of Lisbon. I stole your car and I sent you a warning on the roll wrapping through my waitress friend."

"But you didn't scare us!" Freddie declared.

"No." Manuel shook his head sadly. "But how did you know where I had hidden the tile picture?"

Flossie giggled. "The green rooster crowed and told us where he was!"